M O N S O O N S

a collection of writing

L a r a i n e   H e r r i n g

DUALITY PRESS
5025 North Central Avenue, #444
Phoenix, Arizona USA
85012-1520

First Edition
April 1999

Printed in the United States of America

ISBN: 1-892579-06-5

"I seem to have an awful lot of people inside me."

- Dame Edith Evans

"We are, each of us, our own prisoner. We are locked up in our own story."

- Maxine Kumin

*" It doesn't matter who my father was;
it matters who I remember he was. "*

- Anne Sexton

for
Glenn Alderman Herring, Junior

I dreamed that I met God. She was sitting on a rather uncomfortable looking rock and she was blowing soap bubbles. That's all. No lightning. No throne. Nobody in sheets with harps. No cherubs or pearly gates. An empty field, a rock, and a little girl blowing soap bubbles. Soon the air was thick with floating rainbow bulbs, gliding and merging into bubble-clumps or falling and bursting on the pointed tips of emerald green grass.

Then it happened. It started small and grew like a wave of sound. Millions of tiny voices all at once. Each bubble had a voice, a spirit, which was rejoicing or laughing or crying. Some floated higher or lower, never seeming to touch the ground. Some were caught in the whirl and wake of others as they passed. Some though, fell straight from the hand of God, and filled with the same breath of creation, fell to a sharp, bursting end.

God's voice in my head said, "Choose the most beautiful."

I can't do that. They're all the same. I mean some reflect different colors and lights and some are different sizes. Some last longer, but they're all...

"Choose," she said. "Which one should I not have made? Choose the good bubble from the bad bubble. Or choose, if they should all follow the same course, which one it should be. Would they be more wonderful if they all floated single file to the very same end? Or is there perfection in this chaos?"

from *Shark Bytes* by J.B. Hartgraves

reprinted with permission from the author

CONTENTS

Earth

Water

Fire

Air

A version of "Salt Mines" originally
appeared in *The Bohemian Chronicle*, 1994

"Monsoons" originally appeared in *Walking the Twilight: Women Writers of
the Southwest*, ©1994, Northland Press

"Boundaries" originally appeared in *i.e. magazine*, 1996

Earth

*"To move freely,
you must be deeply rooted."*

- Bella Lewitzky

Wilmington, NC

Wilmington shouts to me from her ivy covered plantations
Screams to me of midnight lynchings
Sunrise Sunday services
Ripe red tomatoes.

Wilmington howls through ancient oaks
Chirps through bluejays
Sits heavy and thick on crumbled tombs
And stirs the dead awake.

Wilmington snakes through my veins
Crystalizing my arteries
Choosing which breath comes in
Which breath goes out.

Wilmington oozes black honey
Black blood
Turns my lungs inside out
And wakes my stomach up.

Wilmington tickles me under the chin
And rubs her salt air in my wounds
And laughs
As I spin spirals through my cobwebbed history

Ending, again, at the beginning.

Sugar

$\mathcal{M}$andy wondered exactly when she forgot the sound of his voice. She couldn't pinpoint the exact moment. She had always been certain it would never happen.

She stood on the gray, wooden porch watching a black widow slowly construct its web. Daddy used to sit here on this very porch, watching a different black widow building a different web, on a different day. He probably sat looking at this creek, wondering what would happen in his life. Probably sat until dark, until the black widows disappeared and the lightning bugs reappeared. Probably oblivious to the mosquitoes, just like Mandy was now. She gazed at a tiny one on her freckled forearm, back legs hunched in two perfect forty-five degree angles, drinking her blood. She didn't even try to brush it away. His voice. When did she lose his voice?

That voice had followed her everywhere. He had imprinted it in her brain, forever, she had thought. She could drive down I-40 and hear it on the radio, a deep baritone in between Don Henley and "a little Elvis for you veteran rock and rollers." She could hear it at work. "Don't settle, sugar. Don't settle." Sometimes she could even hear it when she was making love. "Do you love him, sugar? Do you?" It did wonders for the mood, and she always felt a little irritated, but she never thought she'd lose that sound. Never in a million years.

Daddy died four years ago. Not sudden, not unexpected, but quite dead nonetheless. Mandy had tearlessly watched them make the sign of the cross over the coffin and lay him in the ground. She didn't cry until she was in the car, and only then behind mirrored sunglasses. "I will not cry for you again," she stoically promised herself. And she never did. On the outside. Sometimes she caught herself talking about him as if he were alive. For a while, in the murkiness of her mind in the early morning, she had picked up the phone and begun to dial his number before she remembered. But that was only because that voice followed her everywhere.

The front screen door clapped, startling her. "Mandy? You home?"

It was Gary. He was the latest in her string of boyfriends/ live-ins. Overall, he was probably the closest to the ever elusive Mr. Right she'd found yet. He was an official Artist/Sculptor/ Educator. They had met when Mandy applied for a modeling position to earn some extra money. She had been both flattered and aroused at the prospect of posing nude for the sake of art. Of course, he didn't stay a stranger long. He had large, sensitive hands. Mandy adored hands, and the strips of blue-gray clay under his nails only added to her excitement. An artist at work—and at work on her, no less. "Out here!" She turned away from the creek.

"Whatcha thinking about, kid?" She noticed a clump of

brown clay in his already dishwater blond hair. She plucked it expertly from the strands and rolled it between her fingers.

"My Daddy's dead."

"Yes..." Gary's caterpillar eyebrows moved closer together as he waited for Mandy to continue.

"No, I mean he's really dead."

"Did you start drinking without me?" He grinned, and turned to go into the house.

"No! I mean—I don't know what I mean. Something's gone today. Something that was here until—I don't know when —is gone now."

"Honey, why don't you come inside." Mandy snapped her arm away from his patronizing grasp, but she allowed herself to be directed into the dining room. Gary brought her a glass of iced tea, sweetened with just a dab of the store-bought lemon juice she liked, and sat beside her on a redwood chair. "I'm not trying to be insensitive here—"

Mandy cut him off. "Make love to me." He stared at her. "I mean it." She quickly changed her tone, unaware of where this desire came from, certain only that she wanted him. "Please." She pressed her hands against his chest. Gary kissed her, his tongue travelling inside her mouth. She usually didn't like that, but she didn't push him away this time. She opened her mouth wider, anticipating his touch between her legs.

She didn't make a sound when he entered her; she just pulled him closer, deeper. As he thrust faster, she listened harder for the voice. "Do you love him, sugar?" But it didn't come. She heard only Gary and her own final sounds.

"You OK?" Gary said, running his thumb and forefinger over her breast. She nodded, relaxed, and felt her nipples rise again.

A few days later, Mandy lay propped up against two tur-

Laraine Herring   *17*

quoise floor pillows. "Can you spread your legs just a little?" Gary called from across the room.

"Not and stay still for three hours!" Mandy shifted the pillows and posed again. "Better?"

"Mmmmmmm. Much." He put the blade back in his mouth.

She was amazed at how casual this whole posing thing had become to her. She never even thought about being nude anymore. She vaguely wondered if that was good or bad. "What's this one for?"

"Just for class. I promised the kids I'd bring in some of my work. This won't take much longer. I'm just doing a rough outline. It's only first year."

"Mmmmhmmm." Gary taught art at the University of North Carolina at Wilmington. It was quite a step for this Baptist town to allow a man with such "pornographic" work to set up shop here. He took the job at the college because no one was buying his work for the immense art value Gary felt was there. He had been disappointed, but Mandy was glad for the steady income because she'd be free to work on her novel. She'd made little progress lately and she knew Gary was getting frustrated with her.

"I can't write *War and Peace* overnight!" she had screamed, when for the ninth day in a row Gary had come home to find her sitting on the porch staring at the creek.

"I'm not talking *War and Peace*! Just a sentence or two! Even a word!" The slam of the screen door had made her jump as he stalked back into the house.

The truth was she couldn't write without that voice. The silence scared her. Maybe all her talent had come from Daddy. Maybe she wasn't capable of writing without his direction. "Ridiculous!" she had said, picking at her peach nail polish. "You're being ridiculous." He's been dead four years. Four! That's not yesterday. That's not even last year. She felt there was something irrational about the way she rationalized Daddy's death. But she missed him. She felt as if she never missed him before now, and she didn't know how to explain it to Gary.

Gary was an atheist, and until Daddy died, she had considered herself a confirmed agnostic. But once he was gone she had an overwhelming need to believe that he still lived somewhere. That was when she discovered the secret of religion. Religion fuels the guilty and the grieving. Doesn't serve much other purpose except taking up land that could be turned condo. Lately her belief in Jesus had travelled the way of the Sweet By and By with Daddy.

Today she felt empty, not only like she'd lost someone she loved, but also like she'd lost part of herself. Maybe all of herself. That was the scary part. Had she built her entire identity around a ghost? Had it gone on so long that she couldn't get herself back? She felt herself pushing Gary away but seemed powerless to do anything about it.

When Gary came home, he found her in her usual crouched position on the porch. "Do anything today?"

She looked up from her kneecaps, but did not meet his gaze. She was almost there. Inside herself she had almost found it—almost heard his voice. Damn him for interrupting her! When she didn't respond, he went back into the house and down to the basement to work on another piece. Not of her, though. He'd found another model. A young girl, nineteen, from his class. Mandy thought her name was Sue. "She's just a student, Mandy. Just temporary, 'til you feel up to modeling again." Gary was probably telling the truth, now. But it wouldn't be the truth for much longer if Mandy didn't straighten herself out.

She walked onto the rickety pier. Rolling off her pink

slouch socks, she plunged her legs into the thick water. A heron stood in the marsh, looking for fish. Mandy wondered how much the water had moved when Daddy had put his feet into the swamp. She remembered he'd said an alligator used to live here.

Her thoughts wandered to her abandoned novel. Lester, the protagonist, and also her favorite character, was just about to sell one of his paintings to a prestigious gallery in New York City when she had stopped writing. She absently wondered if Lester missed her. She knew how anxious he was to sell a painting. Maybe now he could retire from the advertising job he hated so much. She closed her eyes and began to picture Lester—nerdy, black-rimmed glasses, scraggly hair—unlike Gary, paint stained the underside of his nails. The warm water surrounded her toes as Lester took shape, strutting down a busy street...

When Mandy opened her eyes, it was dark. The heron was gone and she couldn't feel her feet.

"Gary!" she screamed, running barefoot down the pier. "Gary!" She ran down the stairs to the basement, shutting off the Led Zeppelin Gary had blasting on the CD player. "Gary," she was panting now, standing in front of him, wet bare feet, arms and legs swollen with mosquito bites.

"Hmmmm?" He didn't look up. He was concentrating on cutting the clay stomach of this nineteen-year-old Sue.

"Please—" her voice cracked and she felt tears from four years ago clutching at the back of her throat. "I'm sorry, Gary." She hardly heard the words herself.

"What?" He looked up from his work.

"I'm sorry. I—" The tears rushed past her eyes as if her eyeballs were not there. She licked her lips and her tongue became coated with salt. "It's just that—my Dad died, Gary. He died and—"

Gary held her close, leaving wet, silvery clay hand prints on the back of her T-shirt. "I love you," he said, kissing each of her eyelids.

She sniffed. This time, the only voice she heard was her own.

Preacher Girl

$\mathcal{I}$ first felt the presence of the Holy Spirit in Miss Hemphill's fifth grade social studies class, right in the middle of Joleen Hick's Mt. Vesuvius presentation. Joleen was explaining how, in 79 A.D., the lava had spread so quickly through Pompeii that people literally became statues as the molten liquid rushed over them. I was watching her brown ponytail bob up and down with her excitement, when I suddenly felt a warm tingle somewhere around my lower abdomen. At first I thought I had to pee, but the hot waves travelled through my body so intensely that when they reached my brain I leapt up from my chair screaming, "Praise Jesus!" just like Reverend Walker did every Sunday at the First Free Will Baptist Church of New Hanover County.

Joleen Hicks kicked her volcano model and started to cry. Miss Hemphill said that it was all very fine that I had a personal relationship with the Lord, but I needed to learn to keep my enthusiasm under control. "Make a joyful noise!" I insisted and then she insisted that I sit out in the hall until I could work out a less disruptive way of communicating with our Savior.

The hall seemed unusually long and quiet. The brick walls were painted that bizarre mix of green and yellow that splattered every grade school south of the Mason-Dixon. I pulled my knees up to my chin like they taught us to do in the tornado drills. "Thank you, Lord Jesus," I prayed. "I'll find a way."

I was chosen! God had reached down from the glorious heavens and chosen me to fill with the Spirit, His saving Grace! And now it was up to me. I had a sacred and solemn duty. I had a purpose. I was called to be a Savior of Souls and I was above the rules and laws of average folks. So I got up and left the school.

Out in the salty midmorning air, I saw the world with new eyes, heightened, I was sure, by my personal connection to sweet Jesus. I picked a dandelion and inhaled so deeply I was sure I could smell the Atlantic before I blew the seeds to kingdom come. Mama was surprised when I showed up in the middle of "All My Children."

"You sick?" she asked, not looking away from the screen.

"No, Mama. I felt the Holy Spirit move inside me just like Reverend Walker said."

"That's nice, dear. Want a tuna fish sandwich? Commercial's comin'."

"No, Mama. I think I'll fast like Jesus in the desert."

"Jesus fasted forty days, love. You be sure and eat before then."

"Yes, Mama." I rushed upstairs to my Bible. This was turning out to be a monumental year for me. I had already faced and survived the trauma of reaching double digits. I had solemnly blown out the ten candles on my chocolate layer cake, knowing that I quite possibly would never reach one hundred and therefore never experience such a "rolling over" of the numbers again. Now, Jesus had personally spoken to me and given me his Holy Spirit and I was assured of everlasting peace and salvation according to Jesus' very words.

I had been increasingly worried about an eternity in the fiery pit of hell, basically ever since I'd begun listening more intently to Reverend Walker. The good Reverend became possessed with the Spirit every Sunday morning and I was sure he could see inside my soul at all the sins I had committed that week. If Reverend Walker could see, then God could see, and if that was true then I would surely burn.

Christianity has very simple rules. I broke many of them all the time. The sins of Pride and Jealousy. And I often thought perfectly terrible things. I wished people dead. Joleen Hicks especially because of that time she pushed me off the monkey bars on the playground. That's why it was a particular relief that I was touched during her social studies project. It was a sign. The Lord was on my side. I would be forever safe. I would be going to heaven and Joleen Hicks would not. That's what God says. "Many are called, but few are chosen." I now stood with the few. My solemn duty would be to bring others to the flock, knowing not all would make the cut. I stood proud. Pride is a sin, of course. But it's only logical to experience a little bit of arrogance when you've been handpicked by God. Surely, He could understand that.

When I told my big sister Celia, she told me that I must have had an orgasm. Girls can have them on their own, she'd said. I was shocked. I didn't even know what an orgasm was, and when Celia pointed to her private parts I ran out of her bedroom, firmly resolved to pray extra hard for my sister that night.

After all, how would it look if a member of the chosen one's family ended up roasting in the fiery pits of hell?

The summer I turned fourteen, I met Turner Casey. He'd just moved into Hanover from Roanoke. Everybody wanted to get to know the city boy, so in good Southern fashion, the town kept the Caseys so busy the first month they were in town with socials and barbecues and all around visitin' that I hardly got the chance to say "Praise God" to him. I knew I had to get to him soon because everybody knew Roanoke was overrun with Methodists. I had to make sure to get him to Free Will Baptist before it was too late for his soul.

Reverend Walker said the Methodists didn't even dunk! And everyone knows they use real wine at their Lord's Supper. I know that for a fact because my Mama caught Reverend Peterson from St. John's Methodist in line at the Food Lion buying twelve bottles of merlot. Twelve bottles! You give me one other good reason why a pillar of the community would be buying twelve bottles of merlot on a Saturday afternoon. Believe me I tried, wanting to give the benefit of the doubt and all, but, as my Grandma Boggs says, there aren't two ways to look at evil. She's right too. There's only one side to everything and that's the side of God. Not too hard to figure out what side that is if you got any sense at all.

Well, the time finally came around for Mama to have the Caseys over for tea and tomato sandwiches. All morning Mama grumbled. She grumbled on the way to Food Lion, she grumbled in the checkout line, she grumbled all the way home and she even grumbled cutting up the tomatoes (and that's the best part because you get to see the inside face of the tomato). Mama was never much for the social scene of the good Southern woman. "I got much better things to do with my time then give away perfectly good food and conversation to a bunch of strangers." I imagined that those better things entailed watching "All My Children" or maybe Sally Jesse, but I guess maybe I'm not being fair. Mama thought the Caseys were Yankees anyway. To her, Virginia was as far north as Canada, and not the Father, Son, or Holy Ghost could convince her otherwise.

Mama had just finished putting the tomato slices in a dish and was starting on the cucumbers when they pulled up in their clunker of a pickup. "Lands sakes, they're going to leave tire tracks on my marigolds," Mama said under her breath before she flashed her down-home smile. "Welcome! Won't ya'll come in?"

Well, while Mama was on her best behavior for Mrs. Casey, Turner got restless and poked around Mama's china cabinet. I could tell Mama was getting a bit nervous even while she played the perfect hostess, and truth be told, so was I. How could we be sure this strange boy wouldn't dare to touch one of the plates or cups? To this day, I swear I think the world would just stop dead on its axis if someone touched Mama's china. Luckily for Turner and all the other creatures great and small, Mrs. Casey suggested we go outside and play in the backyard until lunchtime.

I was quite insulted at the idea of being sent out to "play" at my age, and I was shocked that my great spiritual aura did not cause Mrs. Casey to see that I was special, but I did want to be alone with Turner so I could check out what kind of plan he'd come up with for his afterlife. Turner, quite obviously relieved to be freed from the house, bolted into the backyard.

"You know, the polite thing to say is excuse me when you leave the room." I said.

He stared at me like I had my ears pierced. "Excuse me!" He stuck out his tongue.

Oh, that's good, I thought. He's going to take more work

than I imagined. Satan might be already carving out a cell for him now. I had to act quickly so I cut to the chase. "What are your plans after death?"

"What?" He picked up an acorn and rolled it between his fingers. "Leave me alone."

"I can't. I've been chosen by God."

Turner laughed at me! I didn't know what to do! No one ever laughed at me. Especially not after I told them our Lord had called me. Looked like folks were right when they talked about the Methodists. I'd had no idea they were this bad. I thought they were just healthy competition. Like a visiting football team.

"And just what did God choose you to do?" He smiled the smile of the devil and when he looked at me I felt fat and awkward like I did in gym class when I would be banished to right field by whichever team I was on and we would collectively pray no one hit the ball to me.

"God chose me to spread His Word and bring others to the flock of Christ." I spoke to the grass.

"They brainwash you guys young down here, don't they?"

"I don't even know what you're talking about, and you better hope, Turner Casey, that God doesn't either."

"I'm not too worried about God," he said. "Person has enough to worry about without worrying about offending someone who doesn't even exist."

Dear Lord, give me strength, I prayed. Satan had a-hold of Turner's eternal soul so tight I began to doubt even my divine ability to rescue it. "Father, forgive him. He knows not what he says."

"I know exactly what I said," Turner threw the acorn on the grass. "Why are you so worried about me anyway?"

"Because I have to be."

"Why?"

"Why?! I don't know why. We don't always know God's plan for us."

"How old are you?"

I stood up as straight as I could. "Fourteen."

He shook his head at me like I was seven. "You sound thirty."

"What's that supposed to mean?"

"It means you're too young to be so serious all the time."

"Saving souls is a very serious job. You'd be a lot better off if you'd give some thought to your own soul every once in awhile."

"What makes you think I don't?"

"Well," I stammered. "For one thing, you just said you didn't believe God exists."

"Maybe I just wanted to hear your little speech. You're cute when you're being devout." Turner turned his back on me and started to walk out of the yard.

"Wait! We're not supposed to leave the yard!"

"You're fourteen years old and you can't leave the back-yard?" He looked genuinely stunned. This boy was trouble. And he just asked "why" way too much for his own good. Some things just are, and that's all a body needs to know. Just ask Reverend Walker or grandma.

"Well, I mean, Mama's expecting, she's going to have lunch ready soon and I'll need to be close by if she needs any help setting the table and—"

"Oh, be quiet for a minute. You talk too much. Maybe you truly are meant to be a preacher. Never met anyone with so dang much to say all the time."

Well, I'll be darned if he didn't keep heading for the woods. "Turner! Don't go that far!"

"Will you quit being so paranoid? I'm not going to get lost out there."

"Yeah, but there's all sorts of things that can happen in those woods. There could be perverts or wild animals or something too horrible to even think about."

He turned back around and took two steps towards me. "Why are you afraid of the woods? You can't tell me you've lived here your whole life and you've never once gone into those woods? You're leading a very sheltered life for a disciple of the Lord. How are you supposed to understand the lives and problems of everyone you're trying to save if you don't ever live a life of your own?"

"I have a life of my own, Turner Casey. I have a perfectly wonderful life!"

"Then why are you so afraid of everything? Never in my whole life met a girl who was so scared."

"I'm not scared."

"Then come with me." And he ran out of the back fence and disappeared into the pines. I turned toward the house. I could see Mama and Mrs. Casey in the front room. Mama gestured wildly with her hands. Every once in awhile the sun caught on her diamond, flashing a laser of light out the window. They could be at that for hours. As much as Mama acted like she hated "obligatory visitations," she was certainly able to participate with the best of them. What could possibly happen? Mama would understand that Turner's everlasting soul was more important than scooping out the Jell-O mold. I quickly prayed for forgiveness and crept out the back gate.

We were a by-the-book family values family, so it was no surprise when all the Disney forest scenes flashed through my mind. Bambi running frantically through the burning forest; Snow White fleeing the Evil Queen; big- eyed owls and evil trees surrounding her, poking and pecking at her, trying to keep her from the security of the dwarfs' dwelling. When I finally got hold of my imagination, I noticed that the woods weren't really as dark as they were in the movies. In fact, I could see the sun up through the trees, almost bright enough to warm me.

"See?" said Turner, pointing straight ahead. "You can see them houses out there. You ain't far from anybody. Not like we're charting new territory in the rain forest."

I could indeed see the chimneys from the development across the creek. Some of the chimneys blew pale blue smoke toward the sun. Some of them looked like they hadn't seen fire since the Depression. "I won't have you makin' fun of me. Just because a body is content don't mean he's a fool."

"I never said you're a fool. You're just simple. And afraid. Don't you think God will protect you?"

Truth be told, I hadn't thought too much about it. I figured I'd just have sense enough to stay away from bad situations and God could save His energy. "A fool and his money are soon parted."

"What? Think you've got the wrong quote there, sister." He poked me in my ribs. "Believe it or not, we do have the Bible in Virginia."

Well, I was so mortified I thought I'd just let that slide. After all, it was the wrong quote. Suddenly, Turner looked cute standing in the patch of sunlight, kicking at a pile of mildewed leaves, his blue eyes glinting like a coon's. "So why'd ya'll move down here?"

"My Daddy got a job at the textile plant. He's the assistant plant manager."

"Wow." I kept staring at him while I tried to act like I wasn't staring at him. When he caught me, I just pretended like I was sizing him up for Jesus. "Do you like it here?"

"'S'alright. Sure is different down here though. Ya'll don't seem to relax. Take everything so serious."

"God is very serious."

"No, He's not. Look at all the crazy things He's done. Like whirlpools and platypuses and caterpillars. Look at your own self! You're pretty goofy too. All of us is. They say we're made in his image, so God must be kinda goofy too, don't ya think?"

I never thought about it that way. Platypuses were kind of silly animals. They couldn't help it. Maybe that's why folks don't mention it. It just wouldn't be proper.

"I want to kiss you, preacher girl." Turner moved towards me and I backed away right into a long leaf pine. "You ever been kissed before, preacher girl?"

Well, I hadn't, and I most certainly was not going to experience my first kiss in some dark woods with a heathen Yankee. "How old are you?" I asked.

"Sixteen."

"That's old enough to go to hell."

"There's an age requirement?"

Suddenly I felt that warm tingling feeling I felt in Mrs. Hemphill's class. Turner smelled like Skippy peanut butter and his lips were stained a little pink from Kool-Aid. He kissed me quickly on the mouth.

"There, preacher girl. That wasn't so bad, was it?"

"Your lips are dry!" I screamed and wiped my mouth with the back of my hand. "How dare you! Turner Casey, how dare you!" And I slapped him as hard as I could. Turner took a step back and started laughing. The madder I got, the harder he laughed.

"I'm not going to hurt you, preacher girl. I just wanted you to know you're alive."

"When a girl says 'no', she means NO!" I wasn't exactly

sure what that meant, but Celia always walked around the house chanting it like a psalm.

"You ain't never said no." He took off running through the woods back towards the house. "Last one there's a rotten egg!" He laughed like a man possessed. Not that I had first-hand knowledge of what a possessed man sounded like, but a body can figure.

I was just going to have to be a rotten egg. No gettin' around it. Mama'd be mad because I wasn't there to help fix lunch and I took off into the forbidden woods after some northern hooligan. I'd failed at my mission too. Not only was Turner not chosen, but I didn't think he was even called. There was nothing I could do for him. I had failed God.

Back at the house, Mama didn't say word one to me. She made a point of saying over and over that she'd prepared this fine meal all by herself and we should all be grateful. I got the picture. But Mama'd sooner die than lose control in front of company, so lunch went on like I was a model child and everything had gone according to plan. Turner winked at me several times during the meal. Even once during the blessing! He did have pretty eyes. Blue like heaven.

After the good-byes and we-must-do-this-again-real-soons, I fled upstairs with Mama close behind.

"Where'd you run off to, child?"

"I don't want to talk about it." I covered my face with a pillow.

"Well, you best want to talk about it. What happened between you and that boy? He was makin' gaga eyes at you all during lunch."

"I couldn't save him."

"Lord, child, you can't save a man."

"What?"

"Never mind. What you trying to save him from?"

"Himself. He said he didn't believe in God and I wanted to save his soul."

"Only God can save souls. You need to get this crazy notion out of your head that you're some sort of prophet."

"But I am, Mama. God called me. I have to answer. It's the only way."

"There's many ways to serve God besides bein' a preacher. Maybe another way might appeal to you more."

"There is no other way. I'm sure of it." I looked square into Mama's eyes. "He kissed me."

Mama almost laughed, but she turned it into a cough. "Did you want him to?"

"I don't know."

"Well, what did you think?"

"I think he eats peanut butter for breakfast."

This time Mama did laugh at me and for a split second I hated her. "Nothin' wrong with experimentin'. You just make sure you're in enough control to stop before it gets too far."

"What's too far?"

"You'll know." And with that pronouncement, she left my room.

I'll know. How will I know? I thought I knew exactly what I was doing with Turner, but I didn't. Maybe God doesn't know either. Wouldn't that put me in a predicament? I had discovered that God was often very selfish — hoarding all the information for himself all the time. How is a person supposed to continue on the chosen path if there aren't answers readily available when there are questions?

I broke down one day and told Celia. She barely made eye contact with me in the mirror. I think she was afraid she might poke out her eyeball with her mascara wand.

"It's no big deal," she said, applying turquoise blue liner to her eyelids.

"But I don't think I want to marry him."

"Who says you have to marry him? Mama would just die if she thought you were talkin' about marrying a boy just because you kissed him. What you want to be married for, anyway? I thought you were a preacher." She rolled her turquoise-rimmed eyes.

"I don't know what I want anymore. I know I don't know and that's about it."

"Not a very wise messenger of God, are you?"

"I just don't know what He's got planned for me, Cel. I pray and I pray for a sign and I don't ever get anything. It's like He's not there at all."

"Welcome to reality. Glad to have you back. None of us knows what God wants. Most of us aren't sure there is one. We just keep going on day after day. Just kinda tryin' our best, you know? None of us has a road map, sis. You try and make everything so simple all the time and it's not."

"Cel, what's a French kiss?" I crossed my legs and waited for what I was sure was the inevitable answer. I was sure I'd done the unspeakable.

"It's when you kiss a boy and you lick each other's tongues."

"Gross!" I blurted out.

Celia shook her head. "Not at all. It makes you feel tingly. Like when you said you felt the Holy Spirit."

Celia was so nasty I was sure the Holy Spirit was going to strike her dead right there. I closed my eyes and waited. Nothing. Slowly I opened them and Celia was still there, sitting at her bureau, brushing her hair with Mama's thick silver brush, smacking Dentyne between her teeth. "Really?" I whispered.

"Really, kid. Don't get so hung up on this. It's all normal."

"But Jesus was a virgin."

She just smirked. "I can't believe we're related."

"Show me what it feels like." The words tumbled out before I even realized what they meant.

Celia, always the one to appreciate the importance of good shock value, tossed her hair regally behind her shoulders, took my face in her hands, and kissed me, her tongue travelling across my teeth. I jumped up and pushed her away. "You asked," she said and left the room in a huff.

I smacked my lips together, trying to rid my mouth of her saliva like a bad taste. There's no turning back from this. God was going to disown me. I had misused my power.

I flung myself on the bed and pressed down on my abdomen. I felt the Holy Spirit there again. I felt hot and tingly and then my blood rushed colder than ice cold Coca-Cola from the ice chest. I ran my tongue over my teeth where Celia just had been, then folded my hands and fell to my knees. But the prayer words wouldn't come, so I stayed there on the braided rug from the Family Dollar Store until it was night time and God couldn't see me anymore.

The City Dweller

The forest of pines and oaks and elms that surrounds my grandmother's white clapboard house used to be miles deep. My grandmother remembers when alligators lived in the creek and when she added on the sunporch after Hurricane Hazel had toppled one of the bigger trees onto her roof.

It happens, I guess. The ocean crashes over million dollar summer homes and crumbles them like Mississippi slave shacks. Tornadoes blow through the same Kansas town year after year; the same trailer parks. Folks rebuild. Women clean up and repaint and start new gardens. Always in the same place.

I marvel at this. Why not move somewhere "safe" like Arizona or maybe Utah? This is home, I hear them say. This is the earth. These things happen. Maybe these women know what I have yet to learn. No place is safe. We must surrender to the wind, the rain, the sun, because we can't beat them. If we listen to them, they will help us.

36

I am a city dweller. I make my home in a concrete square that looks just like all the other concrete squares on my block. I drive on concrete to a larger concrete structure where I work so that I have enough money to go to the store and pick out my apples and oranges and pears from bins. I have a small rectangle section of grass in my backyard and I get very annoyed if it dares to grow enough to warrant mowing.

I never knew tomatoes had a taste until my grandmother made tomato sandwiches for us one summer. They were fire red and thick and juicy like beef (aren't all tomatoes pale orange — even green?) With just a dab of salt they had more flavor than any salad in my organized alphabetized metropolis.

"They come from the garden," says my grandmother. Yes. So does the corn and the okra and the cucumbers and the watermelon. She knew these vegetables when they were seeds. I didn't know the difference between bushes and weeds in my new backyard. I had to buy a book to know which leafy things growing by the driveway were good and which I was supposed to poison. To me, weeds look a lot like grass and clover looks a lot like it belongs.

The city is very pretty at night, I tell myself, listening to cars speeding by at seventy-five miles per hour. Sirens, accidents, gunshots. Death has a sound in the city. We don't even think that for every ambulance siren there is a life in the balance. At my grandmother's house, when a siren passes by, the crystal plates are loaded with chicken and vegetables and driven down to the affected family. At home the siren is an inconvenience. A sound that wakes me up before the alarm, evoking no emotion but anger. To my grandmother, the siren is a signal for a change. A new cycle of someone's life.

I am afraid of death. I am afraid of change. In the city, we effectively halt change. We can make flowers grow year

Laraine Herring   *37*

round. We exist in climate-controlled prisons occasionally stepping onto our balconies for a breath of fresh air and smelling something we can't identify, but we know. Spring? Life? It's nice, we say. It's a nice day.

In winter, my grandmother has no tomatoes. It's the wrong season, she says. I have the same shadows of fruits and vegetables I have all year. They're a few cents more in the winter, that's all. When she dies, there will be no one left in the family who can grow okra, who can preserve figs and apples. I used to pity her. Living in a house with no heat or air-conditioning. We convinced her to get indoor plumbing just five years ago. Come on, Grandma, really. You don't have to suffer like this anymore. She relented, but I think it was more to shut us up than because she wanted an indoor shower.

Thank God we don't have to live like that, I would think when I was a child. Thank God I wasn't born one hundred years ago. I have learned my life will end one day. No matter how I live I will die. Because we have distanced ourselves so much from the earth we don't feel her pain as acutely. We can't smell that she's dying. Most of us will die without tending our own gardens. Without harvesting our own vegetables. Never feeling the life within the soil filter over our fingers, black and soft and rich. Never knowing that life is a circle because we participate in it organically, daily. Never knowing that we will be reborn, like our ancestors of the earth, and reborn again.

My grandmother does die several weeks after my last visit. Her friends (those few who are still alive) know instinctively that she is OK. I do not share their confidence. I do not understand the cycles, the ebb and flow of life that is at my center and I look to books and tapes for answers. In spring, the soil thaws and the first splashes of green poke through the earth. I didn't plant them. They just appeared. They knew to return.

I am staying in my grandmother's house until we are able to find a buyer. I find green stamps and war bonds in the attic, old milk bottles and Reader's Digests in the garage. Dust belongs here. I don't clean it up. I let it be. I let many things be. I get up with the sun and go to bed shortly after dark. I am forgetting that Letterman is on at 11:30, and I am forgetting that the news is on at 5, 6, and 11 for my convenience. I feed a stray black cat but she doesn't love me. She's just hungry. I want to think that she's my friend, but I know better. I know she's her own spirit. I let her be.

One morning I go to the nursery. I'm not sure what to ask for and I wander blindly through the rows and rows of plants until an employee takes pity on me.

"What can I help you with?" she asks and smiles. She's old. Her red lipstick doesn't fill in the creases of her lips. Her eyeshadow is too blue.

"Seeds? I need seeds."

"For what?" She's very patient.

"Life?" I am bewildered.

"I know just what you need," she says, and we walk to the back of the store where she hands me packets of seeds — green peppers, squash, tomatoes, butter beans. "Be patient, dear. They'll grow."

"Yes," I take the seed packets. "I know."

Laraine Herring   *39*

No Exit

You're comin' south down I-17 tryin' real hard
to go 85 in the 75
while makin' the bug eyed trooper with his radar gun gussied
up to look like Rambo and Terminator rolled into one think
you're toolin' along at an easy cruisin' pace of 50.

Used to be Bell Road was the outskirts —
horse property with nothin' but zebra skin seat covers
and Navajo blankets for sale on the corner of
35th Avenue with nowhere to go but farther west into
the heart of the heart of the wild.

Now when you're comin' south on 17 doin' 85 in the 75
you start seein' lights and Circle K's and Texacos 45 miles
before you get to Bell Road.
You see a Taco Bell next to a Filiberto's next to an Umberto's
next to an Adalaberto's and you wonder where they found that
cute little Chihuahua to say, "Yo Quiero Taco Bell."

Your Indian blanket is spread out across your backseat
'cuz the backseat is leather and everyone knows what happens
to leather when the car heats up to 165 degrees in the sorry
excuse for shade of the cottonwood tree next to your parking
space at the Mission Gardens apartment complex
just south of Van Buren which used to be the heart of the valley.

The lights of the city pop up out of the dark deep desert like
coyote eyes — 'cept you never saw a coyote
up close and personal 'cuz Del Webb and Fulton Homes beat
ya to it. But you can imagine what it must have been like
to lie on your 10-gallon hat under a river of stars and
listen to the crack of the fire and the howling from the hills.

You can imagine 'cuz you've seen the Pace Picante Sauce
commercials and you know the rest of the world is fascinated
with the wild wild west and you live
smack dab in the middle of it, only the last cowboy you've seen
is some pasty yuppy in a hat from Gilbert Ortega's strolling
down 5th Avenue in Snottsdale in genuine alligator boots and
Wranglers — perfectly creased and starched.

You open your window to wipe off some of the bug slime
that accumulated as you cruise down 17
coasting to a cool 70 as you approach the city.
You see the miles and miles of Spanish tiled roofs and beige
houses — row after row after row like abandoned soldiers
on Christmas morning. You figure a guy can't go out in
the desert anymore and light a fire and drink too much cheap
beer 'cuz he'd never find his house in the dark maze of
landscaped streets — all with the word *Calle* in them.

Laraine Herring   41

No matter. KNIX is heard across five states and as you swerve
left then right around a motor home bigger than your
apartment sporting the bumper sticker
I'm spending my children's inheritance
slapped crooked over Minnesota license plates,
you crank up Shania Twain and think of what she'd look like
in a Miller commercial.

You shift in your seat — after all — you've been ridin'
a long time and you wish you could get off at the
next exit and take a leak and grab a taco at the Jack in the Box,
but they're tearin' up the freeway so you're stuck sittin' in your
hot car gettin' hotter thinkin' of Shania Twain in a string bikini
and gettin' hotter and hotter
and then you see a chain gang pickin' up trash so you throw a
cheeseburger wrapper out the window so they'd have somethin'
to do and then you see it's a chain gang of chicks
and then you see Mr. Rambo Terminator Guard Guy comin' over
to visit you and you're stuck in this gridlock while they raise a
power boom across the freeway
and the Rambo Terminator Guard Guy writes you a ticket
for littering and you laugh at him and he tells you to shut up
so you crumble the ticket and toss it in your backseat on the
turquoise and black Navajo blanket and grin at the Guard Guy
who tells you you'll end up in Tent City wearin' pink boxers and
lickin' Sheriff Joe's ass
and you start to laugh deep down in your center 'cuz you know
right then and there them coyotes had the right idea
and you were gonna mosey on outta the Valley of the Sun
just as soon as they raise this freakin' power boom
and you get a taco at the last Filiberto's before L.A.

Grandma vs. Southern Pacific #3

This morning my grandmother drove her car onto the railroad tracks and sat there waiting—*patiently* no less, for the #3 train to Clarkton to smash her to bits. The whole ordeal was quite a mess; her dismembered body was strewn across the tracks; her car, accordioned and steaming, resting, hood open, dead.

I was called to the scene as soon as the cops could ID the vehicle. I remember one officer kept trying to hold me. I think he thought stroking my nipple would be a comforting gesture.

"I'm sorry for your loss, miss," he had whispered to me. Yeah, right. More sorry than I am, perhaps. The men at the accident scene seemed genuinely surprised that an 85-year-old woman would do such a thing. They must have thought my lack of emotion was shock. It was easier to let them think that.

Sorry? Yes, I was sorry. Sorry I wasn't there to watch the train crash through her turtlewaxed Honda and spray her body

43

across a square mile. I was sorry I couldn't have been hiding in the bushes and seen her face when the thought finally registered in her mind, "I am going to die." I hope she saw ghosts and devils and maybe her own younger self darting in front of her as the squealing shrieking engine tried to stop. She was pretending to be Isaac, son of Abraham, sacrificial lamb for Western culture. She believed that God would deliver her and with a mighty and miraculous act of strength, stop the train and save her life. This would leave her even more convinced of her divinity. Too bad, lady. I guess God has no room for stupid people.

I found her shoe—size six Kinney's sale brown loafer—wedged between two of the railroad ties. I bent down to unlodge it; the wind blowing my skirt and cooling my thighs.

"Need some help?" asked the Fondling Cop.

"No, no. I'm fine." Just leave me in peace, I thought. Can't you leave a grieving woman in peace? Ha ha. I'd always heard about people being knocked out of their shoes in car accidents. Seems to apply to train wrecks as well. The police were everywhere and one of the officers was picking up pieces of Grandma and tossing them in a Hefty bag.

"Pardon me, sir," I said. "But that's my grandmother you're depositing in that bag like a dead chicken."

His mouth dropped open and I could almost see his tongue wiggling around in his mouth searching for words. "Don't cross the police line, ma'am," was the best he could muster.

I smiled. "Listen," I said. "If you find her left hand, let me know. The diamond on it belongs to me."

The officer was speechless again. This was getting kind of fun. I walked back to my own Honda. What to do now? I didn't exactly know. I should call Brent, but I didn't think he'd care any more than I did. Still, this was the South after all. Three hundred years of tradition would never let Grandma down in her hour of need. I laughed and turned the radio up loud, leaving the stunned officers with a few bars of Aerosmith.

As I sped away, I thought about how I would answer the various questions I knew would eventually pop up. Honey, why do you suppose she took to driving on the railroad tracks? Beats me. She never could drive. Was she upset about anything? Nope. Nothing more than usual. And the last question—the prize. What did you do to her? I didn't do anything to her. Everyone will think I did, though, and that's OK. Beautiful truth is, Grandma drove her own self onto those tracks and sat and waited for the #3 to take her to her Maker. Perfect little suicide, and it's just like Grandma to make the whole town think it was an accident so they can all mill around her grave and bring devil's food cakes and biscuits and let her soul theoretically pass into the Kingdom of Heaven. A suicide would never have worked.

The truly ironic thing about it is that I know Grandma did not expect to die. Turn of events like these could almost make me believe in God.

"What are we going to do now?" Brent asked me. I was drinking raspberry iced tea and tugging on Haj, Brent's giant black Lab.

"Beats me. I wish I could have seen it happen."

"Sometimes your frigidity surprises even me."

"Very funny. I don't see you buying any stock in Kleenex."

"Maybe not. But she was still our grandmother." He reached for the remote control. Ted Koppel came into focus.

"What'd you do to her?"

"I didn't do anything to her! And I certainly didn't expect that question from you!"

"Better expect it from other people."

"I know. I never should have threatened to kill her at Luby's. I just couldn't take it anymore. I didn't think anyone would take it seriously. Half the clientele is deaf."

"Always the sensitive one."

"Didn't see you spending any free time with her."

"Saved me from having to threaten her myself."

"Uh huh. See how you are."

"Did you call anyone else?"

"No. I didn't think there was anybody to call. It'll be all over the papers soon enough. People will come."

"Are you going to make the arrangements?"

"Me? I think that's the least *you* could do. You never did anything else."

Brent looked up from the television. "Train really blew her out of her shoes, huh?"

I laughed. "It must've been fifty feet from her foot. I think the cops thought I was crazy."

"Not the only ones."

"Very funny. I don't care what you think. I did *not* tell Grandma to take the scenic route home on the tracks and get squashed by the #3 to Clarkton."

"Maybe not. But something had to have triggered her. She wasn't senile, kid."

"I know she wasn't senile." I stood to go to the kitchen for more tea.

"Brenda." Something in the tone of Brent's voice made me turn around. "What aren't you telling me?"

"She drove herself onto the tracks, Brent." My voice was cold.

"That wasn't what I asked, was it?"

"I'm telling you everything I know. Except that the cops didn't find her left hand. That diamond was supposed to be mine. I bet that touchy cop stole it."

"You're insane."

I spun around on my heels and marched to the kitchen, slamming the door. Once I was safely alone, I rummaged in the drawers for an ice pick. Brent always bought block ice. That never made any sense to me.

I really never thought she would do something like this. Opening up the freezer, I started to hack away at the ice block. What'd you have to go and do a stupid thing like that for anyway? Idiotic old lady. The sad part is, I meant what I said in Luby's. I just knew I'd never have the guts to do it.

My grandmother was evil in the most Christian way possible. She went to church twice a week, three or four times if it was a holy week. She grew, cooked, canned, preserved and brought food to the less fortunate. She made the obligatory phone calls to the sick and always gave 10% on Sunday morning, more if she thought the preacher was watching.

But sometimes I think only Brent and I knew her for who she was. She'd had the whole world fooled—and those that she didn't have fooled were already dead. She could make you feel like you're the most important person in the world while at the same time picking away at your self esteem until there was nothing left. Her love was so conditional, with different conditions daily. She was worse than the weather report in Charleston. You knew it was bound to rain at some point so you'd better take an umbrella just to make sure.

Before my mother died, she'd tried to help me forgive

Grandma. She thought that everything she had done was for love, no matter how twisted and warped. My mother could forgive Judas. I could not. There was even one time, ten or fifteen years ago, when I actually thought I did forgive her. I thought I could reconcile my life with hers, but that was before I moved back to her South. She returned to my life subtly, under the guise of pound cake and fig preserves. Soon she knew when I left in the morning and when I got home at night. She knew whom I dated, whom I slept with, and whom I cried for. Not one of them passed her litmus test.

Everyone else on the sound appeared amused by her, so I tried to be, but quickly found it impossible. I would dream about her. I would see her red, wrinkled lips in the steamed window when I was doing dishes, clicking her tongue disapprovingly. I would hear her on the radio and on the television. She had penetrated my spirit so much I thought I heard her when I was touching myself. She'd scream, "God is watching!" and I couldn't come. I knew then that I had to do something.

So I went to see Brent. I wanted to know how he had managed to bear it for all these years. He certainly wasn't leading the orthodox life himself. "She's got a ton of money buried under that damn fig tree. I'm telling you, Brenda, be nice." I didn't care if Elvis was buried under that tree, I couldn't fake it anymore.

Truth be told, we had argued this morning before she chose to drive onto the railroad tracks and wait for deliverance. I had decided to move back to Boston. She was washing dishes, watching the gulls over the water.

"Dirty birds," she had said, ignoring me. "Gulls are such dirty birds."

"I mean it, Grandma."

"Now, darlin', what you got in Boston that you don't have

here?"

"Freedom."

She clucked her tongue. "Freedom! What's that? You kids think the world owes you just for being. It ain't so, I tell you. Family's what's important. Family, faith in God, community. You don't have nobody in Boston now that what's-his-name left you. You'd be all alone. A woman has no place being alone in the big city. A divorced woman no less."

"I'm not a divorced woman. I never married Richard and you know it. Besides, you act like I'm asking you. I'm not."

She turned around. "Why do you want to leave me?" The bluntness startled me. I hadn't expected the truth.

"Because you don't love me."

"Of course I do. How can you even say that?"

"You don't even know me. You don't want to know me. I have to hide everything from you because you won't approve based on some chapter or verse you've drummed up to suit your current purposes! You don't want to know what I do or who I care about or what makes *me* happy. You only care about what it looks like I'm doing. I swear, Grandma, as far as you're concerned, I could sell heroin to preschoolers as long as I showed up for the prayer meetings on Wednesday."

It was then that she slapped me.

I lunged at her, pushing her against the sink, Winn Dixie dishes falling to the floor. I had my hands around her neck and I felt how fragile and old she was for the first time. I think she was scared of me. Her eyes were blue and wide and for once she had nothing to say. I thought for a minute how easy it would be to kill her. The power I felt at that moment was invigorating. I imagined a rapist must feel this way.

I released my grip and she wrapped her own hands around her throat. Her hands were frail and speckled, my grandfather's diamond still sparkling on her ring finger. I backed away. "Go child," she whispered. "Get out."

I was leaning against the old GE refrigerator, panting, staring at her. "Grandma—"

"I said go." She stood now, as tall as she was capable of, and for the first time she looked at me as an equal.

I left the kitchen, grabbed my purse, and ran to the car. I sat in the driveway, listening to the engine, staring at the huge pine and oak trees that surrounded her long dirt drive. I could see her in the kitchen, bent over the sink again, finishing the dishes. I finally caught my breath and drove away, spraying gravel into her marigold beds. I doubt she even looked up.

"Hey!" Brent walked in the kitchen. "What're you doing? You're going to catch pneumonia!"

"What?" I looked at the block of ice. My hands were so cold I couldn't unwrap them from the ice pick handle. I stepped away and shut the freezer door. "Sorry."

"Here, let me take that." He took the pick and dropped it in the sink. I sat down at the kitchen table. "Hey, sis? You OK?" I nodded. "Look, I know you saw her this morning."

"You do?"

"She called right after you left."

My fingers were starting to warm up. "Of course she did. I should have known."

"Why didn't you tell me?"

"I sure as hell didn't think she'd get herself smashed by a train, Brent." I paused. "What'd she say?"

"That the devil had got into you. She said you tried to kill her."

"I don't know. Maybe I did. I thought about it. I couldn't,

though. She wasn't worth it."

"She was scared."

"I went to tell her I was going back to Boston and she started in again, like she always did, about Richard and God and the damn community and I got pissed off and then she slapped me, and I don't know, I pushed her over the sink and— I didn't kill her, Brent."

"I know you didn't."

"Can I have some more tea?"

"Sure," Brent stood and crossed to the refrigerator. "She said she was taking you out of her will."

"I don't think she had the time. Besides, I think she took me out last week for wanting to have sex with Michael Jordan."

"I'll split my fig tree fortune with you."

"You're a kind man." I smiled briefly.

We stared at each other for awhile across the dirty table. I wanted to be just like my big brother Brent when we were kids. He always did the right thing, always said the right thing. So damn diplomatic. I ran off at the mouth. When people would marvel that we had the same parents, Brent always claimed he was adopted. The phone rang sharply and we tilted our heads to look at it like caged birds.

"They'll call back," he said, reaching for my hand.

I looked up at him, and realized I couldn't speak. I squeezed his fingers and cleared my throat. "I really didn't want her dead."

"I know, Brenda. It'll be alright."

I bit my lip and tasted the blood on my teeth as my brother and I sat in the kitchen, holding hands, until it was too dark to see.

I was right. They did call back. And they dropped by with their honey-baked hams and homemade preserves. They came in baker's dozens in navy blue and black, with canes and walkers and blood pressure pills. Strong, wrinkled fingers clutched mine tightly. "She's gone to her reward," they would whisper. "Don't cry, child. She's found Jesus." Yeah, well, maybe yes and maybe no. The woman I knew would have no home with any merciful God.

"Sure are a lot of people here," Brent said to me when by chance we were alone in the kitchen. He was arranging the refrigerator, trying to cram another vegetable onto the stuffed shelves, and I was looking for a clean glass to take to Millie Brice, Grandma's next door neighbor.

"No kidding. Who'd have thought? She must have been a better performer than I gave her credit for."

"How are you doing?" He gave up and closed the fridge, setting the butter beans on the counter.

"I'm OK. I don't feel like I expected to feel."

"Me neither."

"Brenda!" It was Millie. "I need to take my pill!"

Brent and I laughed. "Sorry, Millie. I'm coming right now."

I handed the glass to Millie, who was sitting on the edge of the antique parlor chair. She was twisting the tassels on the royal blue doilies on the curved arms.

"Thank you," she said. "You can't keep an old lady waiting. We never know how much time we've got! You young folks don't know. You think you've got all the time in the world. You'll find out soon enough." She popped two tiny white pills in her mouth and took a hefty swallow of water. "You holdin' up OK, dear?" She patted my hand.

"Oh, I'm fine. Don't worry about me."

"Guilt can be a powerful burden."

"Pardon me?"

"I know you and Francis didn't get on so well. She was my best friend you know. At our age, we take that right serious."

"Yes, I'm sure you do."

"It tore her up that you all couldn't be friends."

I stood up. "Millie, I need to get back."

"Don't rush off so fast, child. There you go again. Either too slow or too fast! I remember when you graduated from college. She was so proud, she liked to have died right then! She told everyone. All the time! Showed us your picture of you in that cap and gown with your Mama over and over."

"She didn't even come." I suddenly felt the urge to cry and bit my lip.

"She couldn't. Sometimes things go on so long a person can't go backwards and make them different. So we just live with them instead. Don't mean it's how we want it."

"I don't think I understand."

"Your Grandma — she didn't know how to be any other way. Most of these folks here in this room saw her the same way you did. They're here for appearances." She chuckled. "And food. But me, I knew her. I knew her since we were babies. A lot can happen in a woman's life, Brenda, that you can't begin to understand just yet." She swallowed the last of the water and handed me the glass. "All I'm trying to say is maybe things aren't quite as they appear to you. Only now you can never ask her. You'll have to ask yourself." And with that great pronouncement, Millie went to join the rest of the neighbors at the buffet table.

I sat there for a minute, not quite knowing what to think, clicking my nails on the empty glass. How hard would it have been for her to tell me she accepted me? Her love meant nothing without acceptance. Maybe Millie was right. Maybe she couldn't say it. I walked quickly to the kitchen, smiling politely at the visitors who cast sympathetic eyes my way. "I'll be back in a minute," I whispered to Brent. Before he could respond, I was through the kitchen and out the back door.

Grandma's house was less than 1/4 mile from Brent's place. They were on the same piece of property that had been ours since before the Civil War. I always assumed Brent had wanted to keep an eye on the fig trees, in case Grandma got a notion to start digging in the moonlight.

Her house was as silent as the eye of a hurricane. The sound the door made when I pushed against it was almost deafening. I felt sorry for the old house. It didn't know she was gone. I didn't feel comfortable once I was inside. The dust was thick and the air smelled of old fried chicken, Vicks Vapor-Rub and rotted wood.

I stood in the center of her bedroom. I had never been in there very long before. Brent and I had always been afraid she'd catch us, so we used to double-dare each other just to stand in her doorway while the other one stood guard. The four-poster bed was deep mahogany and the blanket was a heavy navy blue. The bed was made neatly, with crocheted pillows dotting the bedcovers. I picked up one of the pillows. It smelled of rose. I breathed deep.

Her bureau was also immaculate. The only items I could see were a tarnished silver brush and comb set and a single tube of red lipstick. She must have had a dozen pictures on the marble nightstand, though. One of her and Grandpa on their wedding day, unsmiling and stiff, 1929. My father as a boy on the golf team; his confirmation; his wedding day, 1965. Then I saw myself, smiling broadly in a black cap and gown, holding my degree. I slid the photo out of the cheap gold frame. That day seemed ages ago. I turned it over. In her shaky, arthritic script, she had written, "Brenda — On her graduation from UNC — 1987 — Summa cum laude." She had underlined the last three words twice. I tried to blink back the tears as I slid the picture back in its frame and placed it on the nightstand again with the others.

I picked up the shot of her and Grandpa and studied her face, young and strong. Her hand rested on Grandpa's knee as they both stared straight ahead. That was the fashion then, I knew. I looked at her eyes and wondered what she had hoped for her life on that day. What were her dreams? Were they only this house, this town, this life, the life she had grown into, or maybe it was the life that had claimed her. I didn't know. I would never know.

I released a painful, graceless sob on the forbidden bed in the forbidden room and clutched her wedding photo until my vision was blurred enough to make it appear that Grandma was smiling at me, from 1929, from the start of her life.

Boundaries

$\mathcal{M}$y name is Alma. For longer than I care to remember I have served drinks here at Discotheque Angel's in south Phoenix. I see lots of things change here in the dark club with its flashing neon lights. It's amazing the things you can see in darkness that you just can't find in the light. Like him over there. You have to blink your eyes a few times to see him. Sometimes he kind of blends in to the table like the ghost tribes of Africa I've heard about. His name is Juan Raúl San Miguel, and when he tells you his name it gets caught in his throat like an apology. Hhh-wwan. A long, drawn-out, breathy pronunciation that usually gets all the other muchachas hot and bothered in a matter of seconds. Not me. Not anymore. I used to try and interfere. Try and save these girls from his irresistible charms, but after a few years I've come to realize that if the girls can see him at all, they must be special, and I've learned it's best to stay out of the way when the spirits are at work.

You see, Juan Raúl San Miguel is un espiritu — a ghost. Most of our customers cannot see him. Maybe they see an occasional gold flash from Juan's St. Christopher medallion that they easily dismiss as an illusion from the strobe lights and the darkness. Maybe they think they feel a stranger's breath in their ear as they dance. But only the chosen ones can truly see.

Juan always sits at the very last bar stool, cerveza in his right hand, watching over us. At first I was frightened. I thought I had gone crazy, what, seeing Juan again after all these years. You see, I was a young girl once myself, dressed in tight clothes with bright colors, black hair teased and forced into a curl, lips painted blood red, not quite knowing what all that implied, knowing only that I was eighteen and free and going "out" like my sister Conchita had been doing forever.

On that night, my first night of independence, I saw Juan. Smooth as butter, he glided across the dance floor and nonchalantly tossed his gaze across the group of us, a holy man tossing pennies at the pulsing crowds. We giggled and turned away because we didn't quite know what to do once we'd made eye contact. He stopped in front of me and held out his hand. A gold pinky ring flashed, dazzling me. We started to dance and when I pressed my head against his shoulder, I could smell his last cigarette.

"Alma," he whispered, and I wondered how he knew my name. When the first notes of the next song reached us, he drifted away so quickly I had to convince myself that he had been there at all. My friends were wild with laughter as I stood on the dance floor alone. I imagine now that I had that silly lovesick schoolgirl look you always see on the soap operas. I had laughed too. What else could I do? And I looked around for him, but with no luck.

"He's trouble," my friend Clara said. "I hear he has a taste for las blancas."

Jealous, I thought. I told her to go find a man of her own.

"Suit yourself," she said, and I was alone again.

I saw Juan alive for the second and only other time a few nights later on el Dia de los Muertos, the Day of the Dead. The night was still unusually hot, so most everyone was milling around in the streets, dancing, laughing, trying to forget, I think, that we were there at all. Juan was hanging out on the corner with some of his compañeros, acting like it was the coolest thing in all the world to be outside on a hot night doing absolutely nothing. He saw me and smiled (I know he did) with just the corners of his mouth pulling up so his friends wouldn't notice his sudden lapse of concentration on nothing. That slight inconsequential movement on his hardened face, that softening of the ridged lines around his mouth, his eyes, were enough for me to float down the trash-lined street, past the shouting vendors, the whores, the mangy dogs and bored boys.

I searched for Conchita, to tell her my news. To tell her that Juan Raúl San Miguel had smiled at me. That he had remembered me. Conchita was off with her girlfriends, smoking cigarettes and maybe talking about her boyfriend. I saw them, five almost-women, clustered together in the alley behind Discotheque Angel's, circled, heads touching, opening outward like a sunflower.

I don't exactly know what Juan did that made me so giddy after only one dance in a dark discotheque on my first night of freedom. Why one barely-smile on a dimly lit avenida threw my heart first into my throat, and then places lower. Who knows.

I do know that the next moments changed my life, changed the lives of everyone in our neighborhood. Two gunshots echoed down the streets. People screamed and ran helter skelter trying to escape an invisible enemy. Someone shouted, "Inmigración! Inmigración!" but I didn't see the American immigration officers anywhere. I was not frightened of deportation, like some of the others. I knew I was a citizen, dos generaciónes now, and I had nothing to fear.

I stood alone on the empty street and I had a brief flash of a scene from a John Wayne film of a stand off on a dusty corner in a poor bordertown. It vanished quickly, and when the fog dissolved from my mind I saw Juan lying on the sidewalk, curled as if he had just simply been overcome with a desire to sleep and had lain down in the dusk-light, a pool of glistening red blood for his pillow. I screamed and ran toward him, leaping over fallen trash cans and shopping bags abandoned at the sound of gunfire. When I fell to my knees beside him, his eyes were closing.

"No!" I screamed and screamed. "Juan! No!"

He opened his mouth and a thin trickle of blood escaped and rolled down his face like a teardrop. "El gringo," he mouthed, coughing hollow gusts of dead air, then nothing. Madre de Diós, how I cried. I cried until the day of his funeral. No one could console me. You know how it is. Such things that are so important to a child seem foreign to an adult. Little by little, I pieced together what had happened that night. Some of Juan's friends came and told me isolated parts of the story.

"Chica," they said. "It was not Juan's fault."

"We will take our revenge."

"Hotshot gringo. He best sleep with one eye open."

"He said Juan had made a move on his sister —"

"Said Juan had forced her —"

"Disrespecting her —"

"He was here for his sister —"

"'Good for nothing wetback,' he'd said before he pulled

the trigger."

"Not to worry. He will pay."

"Juan would never hurt a flea."

"Juan did not die in vain."

"No more tears, chica, he is at peace."

November 3 was the day of Juan Raúl San Miguel's entierro, his funeral. I believed Juan was at peace because that was what the nuns and the priests believed. But I knew Juan never attended mass, so I prayed extra hard for his soul to enter the Kingdom of Heaven. I wasn't sure my prayers would be loud enough to reach the ears of God.

The undertaker had just begun throwing shovels of earth on his coffin when the war began. Juan's compañeros had fled the cemetery and driven straight to suburbia to look for the Anglo. They found him, and the Anglo family held their own entierro six days later. Most of Juan's friends were arrested and most of them went to prison, emerging ten or fifteen years later, strangers with hard eyes and thick muscles.

Now it has been thirty years and I have come full circle back to Discotheque Angel's. The Latinos and the Anglos rarely mix in this neighborhood, and often they still fight. The police, the Anglo reporters, still wonder how these things start. Ask us. We know. Ask us who serve your drinks and do your laundry and pick your fruit. Ask us who still erect our tiny crosses on your roadsides when one of us is slain. We grow more angry every day and we draw thicker boundaries around ourselves with each white chalk line we spray away with our garden hoses.

Tonight the dance floor is empty, not unusual for Miércoles, for Wednesday. Juan is on the corner bar stool, ghostly fingers pressed against the neck of his beer bottle, black eyes shimmering in the neon light. Sometimes I imagine he is crying for what he has lost. I imagine he has been fated to wander the earth until he can enter heaven. So this is limbo. I see purgatory with my own eyes.

Juan appeared here a few years ago. A guard, a silent watchman over the club. The mujeres who saw the Blessed Mother of God in their yucca plant have nothing on Discotheque Angel's. Juan belongs here. Just as he always has. He sits on the bar stool and scares away the Anglos. Tries to prevent trouble. Tonight, since it is slow, I sit on the stool next to him with my own cerveza and wonder what to say. When I am this close I can't see him, I just feel thick hot air next to me, out of an oven, that occasionally ripples like the blood where he had lain his head.

"Cuidada con gringo!"

What? The thought sneaks up on my mind, frightening me. I don't hear it. I know it. I look at Juan and his image seems to pulse. Be careful.

"Dance with me," he whispers.

He takes my hand and merges with me, his hands clamp around my waist, clutching at my spine, pulling me close. I reach for the stale ancient smell of tobacco, but I only smell my own perfume. I try to lean my head on his shoulder like I did when I was a girl, but I only sink into the depths of him, a never-ending feather pillow. I surrender to his rhythm.

"Cuidada con gringo!" he whispers in my ear. I push myself deeper into him and wonder if this is how a man feels when he pushes himself into a woman. When I pull back for air, I glance at his face and see two distinct tears shimmering, golden drops against his translucent skin. I move to wipe them away and they are wet and sticky on my fingers. He cries out and looks directly into my eyes, his sadness a monsoon, cleansing me.

"Por favor, no llorando," Please don't cry, I plead. No

crying. But I can no longer stop him. With each tear I take him deeper and deeper inside me until he is only a tiny puddle on the scuffed floor and soon even that vanishes into the air and I breathe him in. We are one, dancing. One two three, one two three, as if we were all the world.

The music stops. I unclasp my arms and look for him in the empty bar. Again I am alone on the very same dance floor. I hug myself tight and feel my own tears, sharp and hot, thick as soap, cutting ridges down my cheeks. Juan did not weep for what he had lost that night, no, he wept for what we had all lost, for the boundaries we have all been forced to erect around our lives. For all of us en solitaria. For all of us lost.

Bloodletting

When I was nine I would lie in bed and plan the details of my father's funeral. I would stay up late into the night, holding my black and yellow stuffed tiger, pulling the quilt over my head so I could see nothing and smell only myself and the freshly washed Hollie Hobbie bedsheets. I would imagine the whole service. I seated everyone alphabetically. I saw how strong I would be. I would hold my mother's hand and tell her to be strong. I would tell her Daddy was with Jesus now so please don't cry.

I would imagine him dead in a maroon golf sweater, his blue eyes closed and silent. I would visualize his ascension, step by step, above us in the hospital. I could see his spirit floating in the left corner of the room, a blue throbbing energy cloud, watching the doctors and nurses, straining to stay. I felt him enter my body and tell me he loved me and I felt the jolt in my ribs as he left for heaven.

When I spoke at the funeral I would know just what to say. I meticulously wrote his eulogy and believed that I could touch the mourners deeper with my words for my father than any Scripture could. People would hug my mother, in my imagination, and there would be plenty of fried chicken and yellow cake and iced tea.

Then it was over and I had been strong for one more night. My pillowcase was cold and wet and I buried my face in it to smell the secure smell of wind and sun-dried cotton and feel the comfort of my own tears, clammy against my cheeks. I listened for my father's snoring in the next room, and when I heard it, I could rest.

I practiced crying silently for many nights. I could cry until my eyes were thin as mail slots and make no noise. I could blow my nose quickly and efficiently and flush the Kleenex down the toilet so no one would know I had been imagining again. I would bite down hard on my tiger's tail to control my breathing.

My canopy bed had six white metal bars holding up the pink and white material. Each week I stared at a different bar—memorizing it, accepting it completely into me. I believed that after six weeks of my imaginary funeral I would make all my sadness go away so I could be strong and dependable for Mommy when the time came for Daddy to go.

I thought six weeks was an excessively long time to be sad about anything. I thought I would be ready and Daddy would be so proud of me because I had planned ahead and got my crying over with early. "Very responsible," he would say. "Foresight is very important. Foresight will save you a great deal of pain in this life." Yes, Daddy. See what a good girl I am? I figured out everything. I even made a list of who to call and in what order. I can love Mommy when you can't anymore. I know

I can.

I wanted to tell you at breakfast what I was doing. When you were eating your eggs and I was reading the comics, I wanted you to know that last night I made believe that you were dead so I would be prepared. But in the morning you were always so alive I thought I might make you sad if I told you you were going to die. I didn't want you to have to think about it.

When I was nineteen and you did die, I put on mirrored sunglasses and drove the Buick with the radio blaring. I had indeed learned how to cry silently, directing the tears with my eyelashes away from any non-waterproof eyeliner. But I didn't see you in the corner of the room when the doctors and nurses were pounding on your chest and wheeling in plasma machines with blue and green lines. I didn't see you in the corner of the room when I delivered your eulogy or graduated from college or got my first job. I didn't see you in the corner of the church when my mother remarried and my heart split in two.

And I don't see you now, when I lie in bed with my orange cat, Apricot, and slide deep under stiff sheets to insulate myself from the darkness. Sometimes I pull the quilt over my head and inhale my body and press the sun and wind-dried sheets to my face where tears are hot lava and I wonder, when I was nine, where I thought you'd go, and why I believed I could set the sadness free.

True Companion

The old fortune-tellers down on Grand Avenue wave their hands through incense smoke and say we are all born with death in the womb. Death is a journeyman. A compañero. A partner. When I think of death I think of eyes, soft brown eyes. I think of my skin wrapped in cotton blankets, you know, the yellow ones with duck patterns and the satin edges. And then I think of a gentle burst of wind that comes up from the pit of my stomach to blow out the flame. I don't see death as a visitor that comes to call once, sometimes twice, in a person's life. I see death in my root chakra, hanging out, watching. Death reclines in my hip bones, in my womb, wraps himself in figure eights around my ovaries.

Death moved in when I was eight years old. One day, no death existed. The next morning, I woke up in my pink canopy bed and saw him. He reclined on the white wooden footboard, one leg wrapped casually around the post, stroking an orange cat.

"Good morning," he said, smiling.

I rubbed my eyes. "Hello."

"You're a mighty pretty little girl."

I looked down at my Raggedy Annie sheets. Not me. Straight brown hair. Glasses. A nose that turned up too far. I shook my head.

"Don't be so hard on yourself. It's a lovely day. Look how bright the sun is shining. It's too late for you to be in bed."

I put on my glasses and I saw the sun peeking yellow angles around the slate blue shade over my window. I smelled bacon and eggs coming from the kitchen. My stomach rumbled. I reached for my stuffed tiger with the chewed tail and pulled him to me. I put the tail in my mouth.

"Don't do that," he said. "You don't know where that's been."

I did know where it had been. It had been in my mouth. But I pulled it out anyway, and rested my hands on the quilt. "Who are you?"

He leaned his head back and laughed, and as he laughed, he stretched longer and longer until his torso was directly in front of me. "That doesn't matter."

"Yes it does. To me."

"I've been called many things."

"I have to go to school."

"No school today."

"Yes, there's school today. It's Tuesday."

"Trust me. No school today."

I looked at the clock radio beside my bed. It was nine o'clock. Mom should have been in here already. The bus comes at seven-thirty. I've missed the bus. Now Dad'll have to take me to school on his way to work. He'll complain the whole way about busing. Except this time it would be my fault, not the bus driver's, because I slept too long. "Where's Mommy?"

Death turned pale as typing paper and returned to his original form on the bedpost. The orange cat in his lap slept. I couldn't see the color of his eyes through his reading glasses. He wore a jester's costume, with big clown shoes and a top hat. He would be a tall man, if he were a man, but he couldn't have been more than a foot tall, even with the top hat.

I rubbed my eyes. This was a very bizarre dream. Even stranger than the one when I saw the wolf from Little Red Riding Hood outside my window. No one believed I really saw him, but I knew I did. I had to go to the bathroom. "Where's Mommy?"

"I need you to be very quiet," he said.

"Why?"

"You don't want to bother your mommy now. She's very busy."

"Doing what?"

"She has things she has to take care of today."

"Who are you?"

He clicked his tongue on the roof of his mouth. "That question again."

Tears pressed against my eyelids. My throat tightened.

"You know who I am." He pushed his glasses up the bridge of his nose.

I did and I didn't. He smelled funny, like bologna that's been in the refrigerator too long. "I want my Mommy."

"She'll be here when she can. Right now she's busy."

"I want this dream to be over now." I put the tiger's tail back in my mouth.

"This isn't a dream."

I heard a bird outside my window. I bet it was a robin. I

saw the mama robin building her nest yesterday. Mommy told me robin's eggs are blue with tiny speckles. "I want to see the bird."

"I'll show you the bird in a minute. We can open up the shades and you can see a lot of birds. But first I have to make a deal with you." The cat woke up and jumped off his lap. She looked like a tiny ball of orange dryer lint, but with big yellow cat eyes. I liked cats.

"What kind of deal?" I stared at the cat.

"You have to open up your heart to me."

"Like Jesus?"

He laughed. "I am more powerful than Jesus."

"Mommy says nothing is more powerful than Jesus."

He grimaced, his white skin reflecting gray. "I am."

I wrinkled my nose. "I've seen you before."

"Yes," he stretched his arms out until they wrapped around me. They even wrapped around my tiger. My ears pressed against his heart. "Listen."

I heard rushing water, louder than when we were at the ocean right before the hurricane. I heard wind shouting. It sounded like crying. The noises hurt my heart.

"Keep listening."

I heard the rumbling of the earth shifting and the shouts of the people falling and rising and falling again. "You do all that?"

"I am all that." The orange cat jumped on top of my tiger. "And more."

"Death," I whispered.

"Yes, child. Without me, there is no life. Do you see? That is why we must make the deal. It is important that you understand how critical this is."

"I know you," I squeezed my eyes shut and tried to remember where I had seen this man, this clown, this creature. He smelled old. Like my grandaddy's closet or my mouth after sleep. I saw my baby sister's birth and I remembered I held her in the car on the way home from the hospital. That was it. Snuggled underneath the pink baby blanket, safe between my sister's hands, I had seen this thing. He had been sleeping, fetal position, across her chest. I pointed him out to Mommy then, but she didn't see him.

"Yes," he said. "I was there. I was born with her. Just like I was born with you. I don't come for people, child. I come with them."

He released his arms and I fell back, limp, against the pillows. "Today, your father saw me again."

"Daddy!!"

"Shhh! Be quiet!"

I stuffed my tiger tail back in my mouth and swallowed my voice.

"Your daddy can't come right now. He'll come back soon, but he had some things he had to take care of today."

"Daddy —"

"Child, this is between you and me. Most people, once they grow up, forget about me. They stop seeing me anymore. They stop believing in me. They ignore me and I hate that. Now that your daddy has seen me, he can't ever forget me again. He can't ever open his eyes to the life he was leading again. Nothing will ever be the same. Now, here's the trick. I'm asking you to carry me with you." He pointed to my lower belly and laid his hand across it. "Here. In your womb. I must live there."

I shook my head and pushed his hand away. "No! Go away! Mommy! I want my Daddy!"

"He isn't here. He can't come for you every time you call him. Today, his appointment was with me."

"Is he OK?"

The robin outside my window chirped. "Yes. But you must be my partner. You can save him and yourself. Let me be a part of your life. Then you will not fear my arrival at the end."

I remembered how sweet he slept, nestled between my sister's newborn fingers. I remembered the gentle rising and falling of his breath. The way he seemed to be a part of her cells. Her eyes opened on the way home from the hospital and she saw me, and she saw him, and she patted his tiny head with her tiny finger and smiled. She had recognized him too.

"If I let you to this, then what?"

The cat jumped into my belly button. It tickled.

"You live in balance."

I thought of Daddy. Last night we had steak and Jell-O for dinner. When I fell asleep he was watching *Chico and the Man* on TV. I could talk to him about this when he comes back home. I didn't want him to be scared. "OK," I closed my eyes.

Death stretched out to me, took my head in his hands and kissed my forehead. "Do not be afraid. I am with you always." And as I lay in my childhood bed, he spread my legs apart and slid inside. I hardly felt a thing until I put my hands on my belly and felt his pulse through my skin.

Death moved in when I was eight years old. He rides in the car with me, goes to work, goes to bed, laughs, cries, and makes love with me. I see him with others, on their shoulders, whispering in their ears. I see him stretching out his arms to stop a car inches before it hits a baby. I see him everywhere, except in cemeteries, where nothing breathes at all but the grasses covering the soil of the earth where the heartbeat of life always pulses.

Steps

The steps of Grandma's house
are still the blue-gray color of
ocean silt.
I look out at the creek
where my dad and my aunt
swam with the alligators and the crabs.
My uncle and grandfather
built the pier that withstood
"Hazel in '57"
but fell to "Bonnie in '97."
Off to the side of the house
is the fig tree
where the family believed
Grandma buried her hoarded fortune.
The air hangs in front of me,
a tapestry of voices and faces
long gone to earth and fire
and tall tales of would have beens
over sweetened tea and honey biscuits
and whispers of a meeting in the
sweet by and by, late at night,
when no one's looking but the Lord,
or the Devil
depending on which eye
you think to open.

Water

*"It doesn't happen all at once.
You become. It takes a long time."*

\- Margery Williams

Spin Cycle

Somewhere between "greatgoshamighty" and "material girl" I stumble. Running right along over four foot hurdles, sliding into sand traps, clapping fiercely over holes in one, somewhere the music shifts. I pirouette, strong and powerful, through graduate school where khaki green walls ooze pomp and circumstances leave me soulless. I fall to my knees, head bowed under a glowing golden cross, and beg for light. Bloody broken Jesus never moves. I twist my legs into macrame knots and sit and sit and sit as the voices in my head scream to cover up the silence. The inside of my head is red, speckled with black shapes that run together at the edges. If I tilt my head to the left, all the black shapes fall into one another and I hear a rushing sound not unlike the crashing of the stock market. Sometimes I hear fiddles, sometimes timpani drums, sometimes the cries of Tibetan bowls.

I rise on the balls of my feet and stretch my arms to the

sky goddess who brushes past me, a breath of wind, and knocks me over. I rise again, this time on red milk crates, my arms holding chain-link fences to keep me steady, but the wind does not come again. I retreat into the pose of the child and press my forehead against the earth where I hear the thump-thump, thump-thump of creation creating. I press my belly against her heart and wish and wish and wish that grasses would grow around me, surround me, and pull me into the womb of the Mother, displacing my pink flesh for purple orchids.

Somewhere between the wash cycle and the rinse cycle I am forgetting. I hang dirty dreams out on too-tight clotheslines and watch the sky for storms that may arrive. Or may not. I clap the dust out of rag-woven rugs and sneeze my mistrust over the daffodils.

I look behind me for unseen unheard threats cloaked in black carrying a shiny silver pistol. I look in front of me and create an enemy. The wrinkles on my face trace a web of indecision over graying eyes and lips. The arch of my back bends forward in defeat. Tears fill my eyes and gather thickness and weight but do not fall. I swallow them whole, two-aspirin-call-me-in-the-morning, and lick the chalky residue from my teeth.

Somewhere between the first throws of passion and the last time I rolled over beside you and pretended to be asleep, I have forgotten how to breathe.

15 May, 1998

My mother sits on the yellow sofa
in front of a lit candle.
I, across from her with my drum.
We are singing songs.
My mother is a Christian in her body
but in her soul she flies.

I am showing her ritual.
She knows from church — stand up, sit down
fight fight fight
but this is not our way.
We are singing birthday songs.
We are celebrating friends.

It is her father's birthday.
He has been dead for 20 years.
We sing to him and she is unsure

but then she smiles and sings,
"Kauko," over and over "Kauko,"
his name.

She is surprised the tears come.
I am surprised.
My mother, ever practical, ever calm,
grieves internally
and I see the green glow of her heart chakra
split and split and split again.

My mother carries her pains in her body.
Her thin frame, wide smile, young eyes.
She presses sadness into her belly
where it dances madly in the night
and robs her of her dreams
but keeps her safe in layers of thick wool.

This is the first moment I realize her heart
is ripped apart. From father to husband.
She loved.
She buried.
She wrapped up clothes still carrying the scent of
Mennen and emptied her house.

She looked to the future because that is what you do.
When your bones break you find glue.
You work in the garden.
You work on the car.
You pay the bills.
You cry in darkness.

My mother and I carry the same throbbing
light in our skeletons
we view the daylight through the veil of mourning
and guard with spears of vulnerability
that raw place where stoked fires sear
white hot patterns in our cells.

1943

$\mathcal{T}$he steps behind me are wooden and warped. I stand on the next to lowest board to pull on the light. Cardboard boxes with pictures of red apples printed on them line steel bookcases. White sheets drape over them, and spider's webs stretch from the tops of the crates to the corners of the room. An old riding lawn mower is parked to my left, a white sheet covering the seat and handlebars. Old green Coca-Cola bottles, root beer bottles and cherry coke bottles stand in dusty rows in front of me on a bookshelf underneath a window with blackened panes. Cracks run through the lower left pane of glass. An orange throw rug is at the foot of the staircase and an old pair of green men's workboots are off to the side. A woolen sock sticks out of each boot. The paper calendar displays the Coca-Cola logo and tells me it is November, 1943.

Grandma often speaks of 1943. "That was the year my heart opened and closed back up. All at the same time." Sometimes she'd say that standing in the kitchen in front of the sink looking out at the marshlands. Sometimes she'd walk down the hall, clicking her tongue against the roof of her mouth, saying, "Open. Closed. Open. Closed," as if reciting a sacred mantra.

I don't know as much about 1943 as I should. Somehow in school we never get that far. I know in 1943 women wore pearls around their necks and white gloves. I know people danced to big band sounds. I know that was the year Grandma met and married my grandfather and that was the year he joined the U.S. Navy and never came back to Charleston. My mother was created in 1943 by both of them, but my grandmother was left to paint the rest of mama's picture alone.

Now, I sit on the rickety staircase leading to her basement. Upstairs, heavy shoes echo on the hardwood floors. They carried her body out yesterday, through the front door with the scratched glass doorknob, down the red brick steps where I always sat and waited for daddy to come visit, across the leaf-covered front yard guarded by mossy garden gnomes, across the gravel driveway where I fell and skinned my knee...into a shiny white hearse.

Grandma would have hated the dress she died in. It was a bright, yellow one with huge white daisies. Her "staying in" dress. I walk over to the yellowed calendar on the basement wall. 1943. I trace the numbers with my finger, leaving a track through the dust. I imagine this calendar hung next to their breakfast table so they could make plans together over coffee and danishes. Maybe a tabby cat lay on the floor in a patch of sun. Grandma would reach across the table for Grandpa's hand and they would smile together.

I take the calendar off the wall and slide it underneath a milk crate. "Safe journey, Grandma," I whisper, and walk back up the stairs, leaving a brilliant rectangle of pea-green wallpaper glowing where the calendar had kept time safe and stagnant under the blackened window.

Monsoons

$\mathcal{S}$he is as far away from the fire as she can go and still stay warm. She rubs her gloved hands together and crouches, waiting to feel his touch on her neck. Then she remembers. It was a split second decision, really, and she wonders if it will even make the papers. Here, in the cold black of the desert, alone somewhere between Globe and Albuquerque, she wonders if they will find her. And if they do, would she be hero or villain? She sits now, feeling the jaggedness of the desert through her jeans. Things just don't happen, she thinks. Everything is for a reason. She lies back on a rock. The stars are hundreds, thousands more than she can see in the city. Thousands more than she ever saw from her tiny bedroom window. When she would lie with him, in much the same position as she lies now, she would wait for one to fall so she could make her wish. Always the same forever wish she never grew tired of hoping for.

The silence is consuming, so completely powerful and

encompassing, that the night takes on a life of its own, its thick fingers closing around her neck, lingering, sticky, on her collarbone. The gunshot snap-crackling of the logs in the fire and her own slow, steady breathing...in-out, in-out...as if from a cave, the oxygen and carbon dioxide maneuvering through tunnels, around stalactites, finally exhumed in one long, exhausted sigh—these are the sounds of the desert at night.

She comes here often. Sometimes with him, but that was before. Now she would most certainly come alone. She sits up straight, looking for the moon. Out here, so far from the city, the moon blends with the stars, a brighter, larger orb surrounded by its sparkling children. She loves the moon and she thought she remembers he did too. But that was before. She finds the moon in the east and stares at it, mumbling a little prayer. The moon controls all things, she thinks, from the tides to her menses to her moods. Maybe it could find a way to set her free. The stars are moving now, swirling through her mind. She feels his hand on her shoulder again, she's sure of it, but when she spins around to look, she sees nothing. She feels it again, icicle fingers walking down her spine, fingers pinching her flesh and freezing her blood.

Why has no one come looking for her? How long does a grown woman have to disappear before someone starts to search? She plays tic-tac-toe in the hard red earth with a rock, then freezes, unsure if the rustling she hears is from the wind or a rattler. Snakes love summer evenings, she reminds herself, and tucks her jeans into her boots.

It was several years ago, she remembers, at least that, when she first met him. She'd seen his cockiness as confidence and his condescension as artistic brilliance. His smile was as transparent as his hairline and his eyes were brown and bubbling with good intentions. Women are conditioned to fall for that, she thinks. Unfortunately, the signposts to the perfect mate are hazy at best, like the Magic 8 Ball from grade school, "Outlook Hazy. Try Again."

A coyote howls from the nearby mountain, setting off a barrage of responses from neighboring canines. She isn't so far from civilization that she can't hear the private conversations of the house dogs sentenced to the backyard to enjoy the beautiful evening.

Slowly, during her life with him, she could claim less and less as her own. She would walk into her closet and notice that his suits, ties, button-down oxfords, and wingtips had moved in. Polyester is a stifling, repressive fabric. It behaves differently from the soft swish of her rayon skirts and silk blouses. It is stiff, erect, and always creased. When they made their inevitable decision to separate, a court of law determined that he would make a better custodial parent because she had chosen to love one of her own. Sure, the decision is under appeal, but that could take years. Her daughter Toby might not need a custodial parent by that time.

At least Toby was with her grandma now. She would be safe until she could figure out a plan. The woman is starting to get frustrated. Why has no one come for her? Why did she feel it necessary to run?

It had been a natural progression of events. She witnessed initial action "A" and followed it with consequential action "B." Anyone would have done the same thing. The law has nothing to do with justice.

The moon is directly overhead now. She moves closer to the fire, stomping her feet to wake them up. The air is crisp as new money and she can sense the mountains and the canyons around her, as if rising slowly from the baked earth to surround and guard her. "None shall pass!" She thinks of the Monty Python skit and laughs softly, perhaps because she knows the irony of the words, "I will protect you." Perhaps because she knows she may be her own worst enemy. She remembers something she read once in a magazine, only she can't remember if it was intended to be humorous or factual. She read that the male brain is only capable of thinking of one thing at a time. That tidbit of information would go a long way towards explaining the random violence and extreme mood swings her ex-husband had experienced.

"I just see red," he had once said. "I don't know what I'm doing. Something snaps." Men accept that in each other. Much like underarm hair or 5:00 shadows. Nothing can ever snap in a woman, because, although perceived as weaker, the woman must continually be the strength. The balance of power is so shaky. She laughs again, wondering what it was that snapped in her and how long it had been gone.

She, too, had seen red. But it was different. The sun was setting and as so often happens in the southwest, it pours through all the western exposures, washing the rooms in a blinding white-red light, silhouetting the people and objects in its path. She had seen him, an exquisite black outline, sleeping on the couch. That was how she had entered, as a silhouette, and that was how she crept through his house, on exaggerated tiptoe, like a Bugs Bunny cartoon.

She inched toward Toby's room. The suncatcher hanging from her bedroom ceiling spun around, tossing bright fairy-dust sunbeams across the room. She wished she had a camera. Her daughter's face brightened when she saw her mother, but she had calmly placed a hand over Toby's mouth. "Shhh. We don't want to wake up Daddy. Take this," she placed the marble cat statue she had given her last Christmas in her tiny, sleepy hands. Toby loved this new game and had followed her, noticeably silent, clutching the statue, through the reddening house.

She had parked her green Dodge Dart a few blocks away so the engine noise wouldn't attract attention. Toby skipped ahead an extra few steps while she, head wrapped in an enormous brightly colored Jamaican scarf, kept looking over her shoulder and in the bushes. Once they were driving away, she relaxed a little, allowing Toby the anticipation of McDonald's cheeseburgers for dinner. She felt at complete peace for the first time since the hearing. Suddenly, a frozen panic clawed her throat. She had no course of action, no plan of attack. Mom. She would drive to her mother's house, leave Toby for a while, telling her she's going on a great adventure, like the movie *The Incredible Journey*. That would give her enough time to think. The panic slid from her throat and settled into her stomach. She drove the eight and a half miles to her mother's house, cool and collected, both hands on the wheel, radio loud, but not too loud, with all her mirrors in proper alignment.

Her mother had been surprised, then concerned, when she opened the door to her bitter divorced daughter and smiling grandchild, clutching a marble cat. She had, of course, ushered them in, asking few questions, the exception, "Where's her father?" to which she got no reply. After that, all conversation that might matter dissolved into routine actions.

She knew her mother would protect Toby. Soon he would realize his daughter was gone, and, always a man of reaction rather than action, would immediately drive to his ex-mother-in-law's, banging on the screen door like the Secret Police.

She hears a low rumble and the top layer of earth shifts slightly in the breeze. The flames leap high, each flame trying to best the other before returning to the A-frame to try again. She hears a loud POP! and a lone spark spirals down with the grace of a feather. She sits Indian style, facing the fire. The stale,

Laraine Herring   *87*

catacomb-thick air changes to a volatile, hot organism blowing and spewing its waste in her face. Her long hair slaps against her cheeks like flyswatters, the wind belching like an alcoholic lover. The low rumble peaks, and pale sheet lightning electrifies the mountains. It will happen soon, she thinks, but she does not move. She stands, touches her toes to stretch her back, and waits.

The next burst of thunder growls so loudly she feels a firm tugging at the base of her heart. It is here. The first cold, fat drop lands in her eye, leaking over her lashes. The second one hits her nose and soon there are too many. Her eyes close and the diagonal spurts of water pelt her face like tennis balls. The angry fire hisses and spits sparks like bullets into the storm. It is not enough. Like a condemned animal, the fire whimpers and dies, its spirit rising with the gray-blue smoke. She leans against a rock, her clothes cold, sticking to her skin like too much lotion.

Her eyes open. The electricity is so vital, she can see a panoramic view of the desolation, the rock, and the vegetation. Saguaros stand, as they have for centuries, pointing to the churning sky, welcoming its juices on its outstretched arms. The wind grows stronger until its force becomes that of another human being, pushing her away, into the rock, yet holding her still. Desert dust twists and leaps, pirouetting in the rain, winding up like a pitcher, then POW! releasing the ball of dirt into her face. She coughs. This dance of wind and water and earth stings her skin. Her fire smolders, steam rising from the ashes. She cannot keep her eyes open. The dust is thick and churning, made into paste by the rain.

She didn't know if she had been born "that way." She couldn't remember giving her sexuality much thought. She knew she wanted a baby. A man was necessarily part of that plan. She didn't know it could be better. She didn't know how very empty she was until Melissa touched her fingers, bringing her spirit to the surface like a diver too long underwater. Suddenly, she knew what she had been missing, and before she could take control of the situation, she had been swallowed by it, the decision made for her.

She expected an amicable, peaceful divorce. She got that. She expected custody of her baby, and when she didn't get that, she began choking and scrambling. She pushed at Melissa and clawed at her daughter, further convincing the powers that be that she was unfit.

But they didn't understand. She didn't understand. Her daughter was not for trade. Her Toby was for life—her life. She was her birthright. Her ex-husband, a decent man, could not be a mother. She was unused to the jeering, the cries of pervert and the picketers who frequented what should have been a simple, private hearing. She could not adjust to strangers believing they had a better understanding of her life than she did.

She began to let Melissa touch her again, gently, her nerve endings bruised and throbbing. She wanted to regroup; she wanted to reenter the life she never thought she would have to abandon.

"It's a choice," Melissa had told her after a long night awake. "You have to decide if you really want to make it."

Coated in a tepid layer of dust, she opens her eyes. The rain is cool now, and light, dropping softly on the muddy earth. She remembers forgetting to close her car windows and looks behind her, but she can't see through the layers of black. She's not even sure she's looking in the right direction.

In the morning she'd know. A few white, unpartnered sheets of lightning flash a farewell. She sits in a puddle, not noticing the dampness through her already drenched jeans. She rocks onto her side, her knees resting on her arms. In the morning she'd be dry enough to pick up Toby and Melissa and head south.

Parallel Lives

The cafe serves Italian. The table covered with a red checkered cloth stretches miles between the two women. The waiter appears, writes down their selections with feigned interest, departs. The blonde woman holds her glass of white wine in her left hand, swirls the contents, stares. The brunette woman butters bread fervently, fidgets.

They are friends of the worst kind. Friends from childhood. Friends from a time when life was open and welcome. Friends who knew each other "when", aware that they both have portions of their past they don't share anymore with others. It is the two of them, nestled in a cocoon of past lives and past commitments. They breathe in the same air, exhaling different courses. The waiter returns with the salads. They are relieved, chewing quietly, purposefully.

Something must have gone wrong in the kitchen. It has to have been at least thirty minutes since the order was placed.

Yes, something must have gone wrong. They smile at each other, the blonde and the brunette, and cross their legs.

The blonde remembers sitting up all night with the brunette drinking coffee and eating ice cream, studying for calculus or memorizing lines. She remembers how green the brunette's eyes were then, how strong she thought she was. They would laugh, talk politics, gossip. She remembers marching in a pro-choice rally and how empowered they felt surrounded by other strong women, other women speaking out. She looks at the brunette now, notices her fingernails are uneven, and tries to see a shadow of the woman she used to know. This friend, this stranger, is different now. She hadn't noticed it in the letters or the phone calls. But now it glared at her, across the endless table, in the Italian cafe by the beach.

The brunette wonders what the blonde is thinking, but she doesn't want to ask. All weekend she has felt like an intruder with the very person she has always felt most comfortable with. The blonde has found a man and has settled into a life. An expected life. The brunette remembers the dreams she used to share with the blonde, but more than that, she remembers the dreams the blonde had that she now has forgotten. Maybe I remind her of that, she thinks. Or maybe she thinks I am as lost as I think she is.

Neither woman will speak. The risk is too great. The fear is a comfortable ally compared to the truth. Where are the lunches? Then there could be more chewing, more smiling and nodding. The time would be filled.

The brunette remembers driving 200 miles across the state to be with the blonde when she had an abortion. She remembers holding her and telling her that her life was more important. Her life had to be fulfilled before a child can come in. They were strong. They were women and they were proud.

Monsoons

Life stretched out before them, an undiscovered highway, and they would walk it together. They slept safe in each other's arms, watching the snow fall outside the second story apartment. They would prove everything and everybody wrong. They would make it. They fed off each other.

Almost fifteen years ago, they met. English. Ninth grade. Conjunction junction. It was the beginning of a new phase in their lives. Looking forward, they joined hands. Years now after college, it is another new phase in their lives. The possibility of taking separate paths stuck in the air, a knife between them.

At last the waiter arrives. Yes, there was a mistake in the kitchen. He is very sorry. Somehow the meals got mixed up. He doesn't know how it could have happened. The two women know. They nod. It is OK. They will eat now and be on their way. They smile at the distraught waiter and he seems to calm down. He promises to return at once with sparkling water.

Mmmm. The food is good. They agree. They smile at each other too quickly. The blonde notices a dab of sauce on the brunette's chin. She points to it awkwardly and the brunette wipes it away with her red cloth napkin. The brunette hears the deafening sound of her own molars grinding together. She hopes the blonde can't hear it. The table between them is endless.

The waiter brings the check and two mints. They argue over who will pay, decide to go dutch. They stand and walk out to the parking lot. They have driven in separate cars. They make no new plans. It may be a very long time before they see one another again.

"So," says the brunette, taking her keys from her purse.

"So," says the blonde. She has her hand on the car door.

"I'll call you," says the brunette.

"OK." The blonde smiles and gets in her car.

Laraine Herring   *93*

The brunette watches her drive away, north, over the mountain. The brunette starts her car and pulls onto the highway, south, and turns the radio up as loud as she can.

Salt Mines

When I drove by your house I think I would have missed it had you not said I would. The front of the house was a narrow, anorexic structure, hidden by trees and almost consumed by its oversized front door. I noticed the blue and yellow Argyle socks hanging on a three-line clothesline, the yellow sand bucket positioned to catch the rain in the doorway. I saw your 12-speed by the side of the wooden wall and I knew this was where you lived. I knocked and when there was no answer I pushed on the door. From the outside in the snow I saw your drafting table through the chipped panes of green glass. I saw the anatomically correct male figure and I could hear you playing the synthesizer on the ground floor. I assumed you couldn't hear my knock.

I felt like an ex-lover stumbling uninvited on a private scene. I thought you didn't recognize me when you looked up, your long fingers still resting on the keys. Your jade pinky ring was turned down towards your hand and I could only see the band. I apologized for barging in and you apologized for staring.

It hadn't really been that long, had it? You meant to write, you meant to call—there just hadn't been much time lately.

It's OK. It's OK. I was just afraid that you were hurt. No, no, I never got the saltwater fish tank. I know you said you would marry me if I ever kept saltwater fish. I didn't think you meant it or I would have.

You smiled then, and put on the Moody Blues — *Days of Future Past* is the name of the album, I think. Remember this?

Yes, yes. I remember running half naked through Mission Park blasting this album and drinking Hi-C in the little cardboard containers with the broken red and white bendy straws. I remember you talking about your dream when you were a woman with arms of algae and ran through the neighborhood trying to find your fingers.

Yes, I remember crying over losing a baby and a lover and a father and I remember you said that I would never lose you. You told me I had gifts and talents. You told me I was pretty and that you loved me even though you never saw my breasts. You held me in the tiny sofa bed and kissed my hair and touched my hands as if each finger were a separate individual me. You told me of your Laura and how she died and that you loved her— and that you missed her. You said that if you ever married a woman it would be me and I had said, yes, yes of course I would marry you. I love you. I love you.

You asked if I remembered the desert—the wine and cheese under the Saguaro at midnight and the sidewinder that wanted company. Did I remember the fawn we saw in the moonlight on the side of the road? And did I remember that she came right up to you and licked your fingers?

You said your mom and dad were fine and did I see your paintings when I was in the coffee shop on Main? And then you said I shouldn't have come.

I'm sorry. I really didn't think you would be home and—

Did I want some water? You would have to go next door to get it. Your plumbing wasn't working right.

No. I'm fine, really.

Hold my hand.

I wondered why you didn't hug me.

Don't talk. Touch my fingers. Touch me. Please touch me.

You closed your eyes and when I touched your cheeks they were wet and when I felt your throat it quivered. Shhhh. What is it? What can it be? You didn't look at me when you told me you had AIDS.

My fingers tightened behind your ears and I bit through my tongue. I tasted blood and I thought, I can't kiss you now. I have to wait until I stop bleeding and then you screamed and I screamed and you clenched your hands around my wrists and broke my silver bracelet.

You said you were sorry and I said fuck the bracelet. I kissed your cheek and tasted the salt. You were alive. Living people were salty.

You asked if I remembered when you left for Boulder.

Yes.

Do I remember what I said?

Yes.

I told you you were the only man I've ever loved.

I know. Your eyes were huge and clear.

I couldn't keep you, I said. I could never keep you.

I wanted you to stop me.

You lie! I picked up my bracelet. You lie because you're

scared.

No, I lie because I'm dying and I can't hold you and I can't touch you and I can't tell you how much I love you and how I know you're confused and lonely and scared and that life was easier five years ago. Only it wasn't, kid. I can't tell you how wonderful it was to find a woman with a mind—a woman with creativity.

I can't tell you how wonderful it was to find a man with a mind and creativity.

I wanted to marry you, you tell me. I wanted to be with you forever.

Please don't tell me that.

I wasn't good for you. I was unstable and too confused to be good for you.

Please don't say that.

But I loved you. Not a day went by that I didn't think of you.

Why didn't you tell me? How long have you known?

Remember me.

Why didn't you tell me?! What did you think I would think?

You stood up and turned off the stereo.

Do you need me to go? I asked.

You looked at the floor and closed your eyes.

Will you call me?

You didn't know. You said you would paint an orange cat for me, but you didn't know if you would call. You didn't know if you would write.

I will write. I promise.

Drive carefully.

You picked me up and hugged me. I ran my fingers through your hair and noticed for the first time that it was more red than brown. I pressed my face into your neck and you smelled salty.

I will remember that.

My Wet, Black Heart

I see you at the Blue Lantern sitting under a green, tasseled umbrella eating frozen chocolate yogurt with peanut M&M toppings. I notice your hands, long, thick fingers, many rings, sculpted nails. You never look up from your book. Your fingers guide the plastic spoon, cup to mouth, mouth to cup. I wonder what you're reading that you cannot tear yourself away long enough to watch the sun over the sea or the couple to the left of you sharing a deluxe hot dog in the afternoon sun.

Every once in a while you roll your head from side to side. I feel the popping of your neck bones; I feel your tension start to fall away. I wonder if you're on your lunch break, or if you're off work for the day, or if maybe you don't have to work at all. Maybe you're one of the lucky ones who can just live.

Your clothes are ordinary enough, white halter top and black fluted pants. Your hat is white and the brim wide enough to rival the umbrella. I imagine your eyes are green behind your narrow cat's-eye sunglasses. I imagine they are watching me watching them.

I come here to this cafe every day at this time. My waiter is Patrick. We've become pals. Most of his friends have returned home for the break and I don't really have that many. We struck up our first conversation out of boredom.

"What's it like to work here?" I'd asked. I'd never waited tables before and was curious. Truly.

"Too trendy," he'd said, and we both laughed and introduced ourselves. "A pleasure, Rachel."

I wonder if he knows you, lady in the wide brimmed hat, reading in the noonday sun as if you would lose your sight at dusk. My friend, may I warn you? We all lose our sight at dusk.

I think you see me. Your orange-stained lips press tightly together and arc upward, a faint smile. You know I'm watching you. You know I'm watching you and wondering if you are watching me. I do not frighten you. I can sense that.

The Atlantic Ocean shimmers, a perfect, living body. I wonder what is happening just below the film-thin surface. Big fish eating little fish; algae, starfish, sponges, anemones clamoring for space, flowing, bending like ballerinas in the deep green water. Skeletons of all creatures live in the ocean, bones dissolving, decaying, contributing. Farther down, deeper, the heart of the sea is black. They say there are areas where no light has ever been. They say there are fish and plant species we've never seen. There's a whole world on our planet that we know nothing about. Perhaps that's good. The strength of the ocean is in its darkness.

And you?

You haven't turned the page in over ten minutes. Perhaps you're reading a translation and it's very difficult? Perhaps you're an actress and you're memorizing your lines for your big opening night? No, I think you are watching me watching you. You raise your left hand, two fingers extended, a wooden clothespin, and your waiter arrives with your check. No! I still have a half an hour left on my lunch break. Maybe you do work. Maybe you're married. Or maybe you were stood up by a new lover. You are as deep, thick, black as the sea. I see it in the two stiff fingers, the wet orange lips, the wide brimmed hat.

You cannot be penetrated easily.

There's a sailboat about a mile or so out on the water. I wonder how many people are on the boat, or if it's another solitary journey. I decide I'll be brave and ask you your name, but when I work up enough courage and turn back to reach you, you have gone.

Night now. The same day. I think of you constantly. I need to know what you're reading. I need to know some part of you. I don't even know for certain what color your hair is. You pinned it up underneath your hat. I think it must be brown. Your skin is almond, rippling.

I walk around the courtyard of the Blue Lantern. I'm hoping I'll find you. Maybe this is a haunt of yours and I've just never seen you before. I would remember. The cafe is crowded with laughing people. Happy, coupled, trendy people. Work is done for the day and they are free until tomorrow.

Life is prison.

At least I don't see you with anyone else. I don't like this place at night. Too loud, too crowded. I like to be in public alone, so I walk farther down to the shore.

I can still hear the sounds from the mainland, but they have become background noise. Percussion to the bass of the sea. I love to listen to the waves. I try to figure out what they are saying to me, what I am missing, why I am searching. You probably have your own life. You're probably scraping the dinner dishes or reading a story to your son. Maybe you're still reading your book or maybe you're making love to your husband right now and he's moving inside you, deep, constant, like the music of the waves and you are happy.

Or maybe you're thinking of me, staring out your window at the moon, and maybe you're not so happy at all. I hope I'll see you here tomorrow at lunchtime. I've made a date with you although you don't know it.

Back home in my one bedroom apartment, I still think of you. If you were here right now, what would you smell like? Maybe you don't wear perfume and you smell only of scented soap. The kind that comes in novelty sizes. The kind that's only for guests. I think of you in my bed, on the right side, your hair splashed across the pillow like thick paint, your eyes wide and glowing, your mouth open slightly, anticipating mine. I can see just the tips of your teeth. I want to lick them.

I open my window and the wind tumbles in, tingling the wind chimes, raising the hair on my naked body. I trace my calf muscles with my fingertips and feel the nerves in my skin come to life under my touch. I'm aware of my skin as a separate organ of my body, reaching, reaching, grasping for its partner. I think of you, nestled between my legs, wrapping my legs around your neck like a scarf. I feel your hair on my belly and I smell its freshness.

I smell my life.

I roll onto my stomach and let the wind tickle my back. I imagine hands on my shoulders, temples, hips, feet. I imagine your lips on the small of my back, light as wind and hot hot oil. I cover my head with a pillow and wait for tomorrow.

Almost noon. I sit under a red umbrella drinking raspberry tea, waiting. I am wearing black sunglasses today.

Patrick told me he didn't know you. You never sat at one

of his tables.

I watch the seagulls rising and falling over the dunes like puppets. So beautiful. Did you know they sing to each other? It isn't necessary to think about how dirty they are or to remember that they are scavengers. No wind today, more bugs. I flick a mosquito off my forearm. I hear the sand fleas, but I can't see them. I realize I don't really know what a sand flea is. All these years by the water and I am still woefully ignorant of my climate.

I'm pouring my third Sweet 'n Low into my tea when I see you come in with your book. The almond-skinned woman who reads. This time you sit under the blue umbrella. Now I can see your profile. Your nose is small, narrow, thin. Your neck like a bird's, arcing gently, fluid and precise. You lick your lips and slouch slightly, opening your book. It's a thick book. I can't see the name. Oh! *The Shipping News.* I wonder if you bought it before she won the Pulitzer Prize or because she did. When you turn the pages you smooth out the left page, caressing the paper, making a definite crease in the center, then passing lightly over the page with your fingertips before resting your hand on your leg or on the table.

"She is drinking latte," says Patrick. I smile at him. "I asked her waiter. I knew you wanted to know."

"Thank you!" I want to kiss him right now.

"Would you like me to send her an entree from you, Rachel? It works in the movies."

I think about it. Yes, it does work in the movies, but this isn't the movies. She doesn't know the script I've been writing for her. "No, thank you. Not just yet."

You don't watch the cup as you bring it to your lips. So elegant. Regal. Regina is the Latin word for queen. Maybe that's your name. Maybe Bella; beautiful. Or Felicity. I conjugate Latin verbs when I'm nervous. Amo. I love. Amas. You love. Amat. Amamus. Amatis. Amant. The mind forgets nothing. Not even, perhaps especially even, what it needs to forget.

You're a fast reader. Either that or you have too much time on your hands. Amo te? The power of desire lies in its ability to be forgotten moments after the emotion runs its course. Passion. Passion fruit. Passion plant. A passion for. A passion of.

I do not remember what it feels like to be touched. I don't remember what it feels like to wake up next to a being, next to a soul, but I do remember what it feels like to touch a back. Cool, naked, fresh in the morning. To trace the outline of a collarbone, a shoulder, the apex of an elbow. To wake up the fingers, slowly, one at a time, stretching them out, folding them back, until they bend on their own, twist, roll, dance. I remember what it feels like to trace hips, full, fleshy, pulsing, to trace thighs, knees, calves. To see eyelashes soft as bird's feathers, delicately closed.

Yet I cannot remember the sensation of being touched. I touch myself and find dampness, but no surprises. Surprise is essential to passion.

I imagine feeding you red, wet cherries. Your lips closing over each one like a cocoon, your tongue tracing the round flatness, your throat and esophagus welcoming them. I wonder if you prefer red or white wine.

Are you a vegetarian? Maybe you have a membership at the co-op. I'll go there tomorrow. I'll say I'm your cousin and want to surprise you. Surprise is essential to passion.

The waves scream as they come together with the shore, reclaiming a little more each time, releasing something new. I think I'll apply lipstick. I'll seductively remove the lipstick from its case, twist it upwards like the unsheathing of a statue, and apply it slowly, methodically, and I will rub my lips together and lick them and then you'll notice me.

But you do not. You turn the pages of your book; you drink your latte; you do not look up. I turn back to the sea. The humidity is already causing my painted mouth to smear. I will walk down to the beach and my skirt will billow in the wind, wrapping around my bare feet. My sandals will be in my left hand and I'll run the fingers of my right hand through my hair and look back at the Blue Lantern, pretend I'm looking for someone and when I notice you've been watching me, I'll wave to you to come and join me.

Yes.

I slide off my sandals and leave the patio, walking, sliding across the hot sand toward the beating black heart of the sea. I take a deep breath and look behind me, trying to catch the green glint in your eyes before the sun becomes too blinding.

Fire

*"The heresy of one age
becomes the orthodoxy of the next."*

\- Helen Keller

Spirit Drums

Slap-slap-slapping of palms on stretched leather drums,
pounding ancient rhythms pulsing fresh and fiery through veins
and vessels long laid dormant.
Silver rings and bracelets snap fire through charged air,
flashing energy, flashing spirit.
Slap-SLAP! Slap-SLAP!

Familiar beat.
Silenced beat.
Heart beat.

Slap-SLAP! Thump-thump!
Pounding out the rhythms on ancestor's feet,
on our mother's mother's mother's mother's
grandmother's beats. Dancin' feet.

Heart beat. Pulse beat.
Rising and falling with each breath, each beat of blood rushing
through veins and vessels long laid dormant,
I inhale and exhale.
I hold life rumbling through my cells.
I hold life wrapped around my neck.
I hold life.
I hold

Silence
Never
Again.

Tending The Garden

$\mathcal{T}$he morning I first saw the apple tree, the sun was a little too yellow. It was early. Adam and I had already eaten breakfast. Figs and water with just a hint of orange flavor from the orange tree I'd found south of the eucalyptus grove. I particularly remember how clear and cold the water was.

I could tell you what actually happened, but I don't know if you will believe me or not. I know you've learned a different version. But I have to tell you the truth, because it is all I know. And it is all there is.

Like I said, the light was different. The sun's rays filtered through the leaves and made square patterns on the grass. I saw dust particles and tiny bugs — you know, the ones that are everywhere but no one knows the names of — spiders spun webs in the branches, squirrels tossed acorns to each other in the leaves. The garden was beautiful, full of life sounds. All the elements were there. Earth, air, water, fire. I still felt damp and

110

open from making love with Adam that morning. We had nestled into each other in spirals. I had rested my chin on his shoulder while he slept and I had just noticed that his flesh was made up of tiny fragments of skin, each with a tiny hair in the middle. He found them on me, too, even in the place where my legs come together.

Adam had gone for a swim in the river. He liked to go before the sun reached the middle of the sky. He would tell me of beautiful color wheels he saw in the waterfalls when the sun bounced off the splashing falls and of talking to fish whose bright scales flashed yellow sun back in his eyes. I thought I would go for a walk. I liked the way the grass felt on my feet, cool and slick with morning. A panther would often come walk with me, her big feet leaving dewy footprints next to mine.

The apple tree stood in the middle of the garden in the center of a triangle of fruit trees. I was surprised to see it. If you could have only seen the garden then, you would have known how I might not have noticed it before. The garden was mile after mile of flowers and trees and animals. Mile after mile of sun and clouds, rain and thunder, water and wind. Every day when I dug in the earth, I found new animals, new worms, new seeds.

The panther lay beneath the tree, the shade from the branches zigzagging across her ebony fur. Her yellow eyes opened and closed lazily, watching me, the tip of her tail rising and falling with the breeze. I stared at her tail, mesmerized by the movement, when I first heard the hiss in the tree. When I looked up, I saw the most beautiful creature I had ever seen. Coiled in a spiral, nestled in the crook of a branch, waited the Snake. Her eyes, tiny and black, shined in her triangular head. I knew when I saw her shimmering wet black body that she was meant for me.

"Hello," I said.

"Hello." She flitted her tongue through her two fanged teeth.

"Who are you?"

"I am knowledge. I have been waiting for you, Eve. I have so much to tell you."

"Me?" The sounds of the garden faded into the distance. All I heard was Snake. All I saw was her exquisite, exquisite beauty.

"You, Eve, have been chosen." She uncoiled her body and raised her head, revealing a sparkling hood of ocher and cobalt.

"Adam is in the river. Let me run and get him and you can talk to us both."

"No," she said. "This is only for you."

I turned back to face her. "What do you mean? Only for me?"

"Let me tell you a story." She slid down the trunk to lay with panther on the ground. I settled myself between the giant cat's paws to listen.

"The story starts before there was light." Snake's eyes glinted, reminding me of the way Adam's eyes shone when we lay together in the dark.

"God told us the only thing that existed before light was Him." I remembered the conversation explicitly. I had stood next to Adam by the waterfall. The sun was warm on my skin. My back tingled in the breeze, and cool beads of water spray dotted my neck. A warm white light shone in front of us, so bright we had to look away. Now that I really think of it, we didn't hear any words. Something moved inside me that felt like the purest love I ever dreamed possible, but the words I heard were Adam's. Adam told me the word of God.

"Did you not ever have any doubts?" asked Snake. "How could you be sure that what he told you was what God said?"

I looked away. I had thought that at the time. I had almost spoken about it, too, but Adam had touched my waist and led me to the water and I thought we could discuss it later. I did not hear God as Adam did. I simply sensed her.

The Snake slid over the panther's paws and rested beside my ankles. The panther watched with one yellow eye. "You wanted to talk to Adam about what you heard, didn't you?"

I nodded.

"What did he say?"

I bit my lip until a salty taste rushed across my tongue. "He told me I was talking nonsense. He told me that God had spoken to him — had chosen him, and I could not have heard anything other than what Adam had heard because God only spoke once."

"How did that make you feel?"

I looked up at the sky, through the tree branches where Snake had first spoken. "I felt ashamed."

Snake's tongue lapped the sweaty flesh on my leg. "Why should God speak the same to Adam as to you? You are two different people."

"I don't know." I thought of how Adam had behaved since that day. He had changed. He started asking me to pick his fruit and pour his water. Before, we picked together. He said that God had chosen him, and that now he knew what was best for me.

"But that's not what you heard from the light, was it?"

I reached to stroke the Snake. Her skin was silken and surprisingly dry under my fingers. Her hood flattened for me and I could see the beautiful colors — the turquoise and amber spiral. "No." I had heard color. The purples and reds sang loudest. The greens hummed like the drone of a bumblebee. The white pulsed. "I felt like I was dreaming."

"Go on."

"I felt like I was being spoken to directly. Like I had been chosen."

"You have been chosen, Eve. That's why I'm here now. To tell you so that you don't have to be afraid of what Adam thinks anymore."

"Adam said God made him in his image, and that I was made from his rib to be a companion and servant to him." I found I could hardly say the words. They stuck in my throat and my tongue seemed to thicken and fill up my whole mouth, keeping the weighty words from taking life.

"That is a lie, Eve." Snake's tail rose and fell in rhythm with the panther's.

"Adam would not lie to me. He is my companion."

"Companion, perhaps. But he also has a destiny that is not parallel to yours. You are woman, Eve. You are the mother of this earth."

"But I have no children."

"You will. You will have more children than the stars in the sky, and you will be remembered for eternity, but you must be very careful whom you trust and what you believe. This is a very volatile time. There are many spirits out."

I walked to the tree in the center of the garden and picked a shiny round red fruit. "What are these?"

"Apples. They are quite delicious. Eat one."

"I cannot. God told Adam that we can eat of all the trees in the garden except this one. He said that to eat of it, we would die." I rolled the hard fruit in my palms.

"Again I say to you, is that what you heard when God appeared?"

"No. I heard singing and I saw this lovely color wheel spiraling through me, and all the animals and plants and people were all on the wheel, each one touching another. Each one dependent on the other."

"Why did you not speak of this to Adam?"

"I already told you. He had changed. Pulled away from me a bit. I was afraid."

"You have nothing to fear. You have been waiting for this moment for an eternity."

"I don't understand."

"Come back over here. Bring the apple."

I walked carefully back to Snake, stepping over tiny pebbles in the grass. I lay against the panther. Her thick ribs and steady breathing soothed me.

The Snake spoke. "This story begins before there was light. The life force in this galaxy was just a pulse of sound. Thump-thump. Thump-thump. Over and over nothing but the heartbeat of spirit. The sound was so deep and so soothing that the planets began to arrange themselves in orbit around the sound. It pulled them in and anchored them. The sound grew louder and louder until the vibrations were strong enough to cause the soil to shift. The earth quaked, fire erupted, the ocean overflowed, the sky withheld rain. All these things occurred to shape the world. Behind it all the while was *thump-thump thump-thump*. The heartbeat of the universe. The heartbeat of the mother. Do you know what I am saying?" Snake slid closer to me, shifting her body out of the sun.

I shook my head. "Not entirely. I feel — I don't know — it seems so familiar."

"It seems familiar because it was spoken to you by the waterfall the other day. Only it was spoken to you by Goddess, not God."

"I don't understand."

"All creatures seek balance. The divine heartbeat is both female and male. It is the light that runs through both you and Adam. You two were once the same ray of light. You have been split — male and female — as all creatures are. Male and female souls will seek each other out. A male soul may live in a female body sometimes. And sometimes a female soul may live in a male body. You choose the body that best serves your needs for this lifetime. You and Adam are important. The world will judge you based on things they know nothing about. They will blame you, Eve, for seeking truth, not Adam for keeping truth from you."

Panther's rough tongue caressed my arm. My mind was spinning, but my center was calm and light. I breathed deeply and smelled the azaleas and honeysuckle blossoms. The scent of warm grass mingled with my sweaty flesh and made me heady. I bit into the apple. Its hard sweetness filled my mouth. My tongue eagerly wrapped itself around the apple's flesh and lapped the juice.

"You have the gift of knowledge, Eve. Use it wisely. It will anger Adam."

"Adam should be pleased."

"Adam will be threatened. This is something you must come to terms with. You must be true to what you know in your heart."

A bee droned near my ear. "Who are you?"

Snake seemed to smile. "Men will call me Evil. They will call me Devil and they will say I tempted you to damn mankind for eternity. Who do you think I am?"

"I think you are me."

She slid onto my womb and curled into a spiral, her tail resting just above my pubis. Her head lay between my breasts, underneath my ribs. "Can you feel me inside you?"

"Yes." I breathed. I did feel her, slipping through my veins, curling in my uterus, rattling through my heart, opening my birth canal. "I feel you."

"Lo, I am with you always, even unto the end of the world."

The image of the Snake faded in front of my eyes. She became lighter and lighter and dissolved into my flesh. Her eyes were the last to vanish, disappearing under my rib cage, next to my heart. When I touched my breasts, I felt her warmth.

I lay underneath the tree in the middle of the garden, next to panther, and watched the sun patterns through the branches. I felt a rush of energy through my veins that reminded me briefly of lying with Adam that morning. He had touched me in a way that caused my blood to turn to rushing water and made me scream out. This time the feeling was slower, more deliberate and constant. I felt this rushing through to my toes. I thought I could even feel her tongue lapping at my womb as she positioned herself in a spiral in my belly before sleeping.

When I woke up, the moon sliced my body half in darkness half in blue-white light. Panther was gone. My belly rumbled. I blinked, breathed deep the night air, rolled onto my stomach and smelled the earth. The skin on my back tingled.

"Eve," Adam stroked my spine with a feather. "I've missed you today."

I closed my eyes and thought of Snake. I felt a quiver in my womb and pushed myself up. "I've missed you, too," I lied.

He kissed me, his tongue sliding over my teeth. My body tightened.

"Where have you been all day?" He ran his fingers over my breasts.

I stepped back. "Here, under the tree."

"All alone?"

"Yes. All alone."

"I've been hungry."

"Strange, that you'd say that."

"Why?"

I took a deep breath. "I no longer hunger."

"How can that be?"

"I had a message today. From God."

Adam stiffened. "What are you saying?"

"It doesn't matter."

"Yes it does. I'm sure, honey, that you were just dreaming of the conversation that I had with God."

"No, Adam. It was mine."

He reached for my hand. "Sweetheart, it's been a long day."

"Actually, it's been a perfect day."

"But we were not together. God has decreed that we are to be together. You are a companion for me."

"No. I am not here to serve you."

Adam's face reddened, his eyes sparked. "I have told you the word of God. Do you dare to disobey God?"

My belly quivered. "I dare to disobey you."

"God will banish you from the garden!"

"God, or you?"

"I — God — please, just come back with me by the waterfall. You'll pick fruit and we'll lie together like this morning. Let me try to touch you like before. Can I, Eve? Please?"

Adam's brown eyes shone. He hardened in front of me. I wanted to touch him, but I clasped my hands behind my back. "No, Adam. I can't."

The veins on his neck popped. "Who is it? Who did you meet today?"

"Only myself."

"What are you talking about?" He took a step closer to me. "It is my right! You must submit to me! It is the word of God!" He grabbed my arm and pulled me to him, forcing his lips against mine. I bit his lower lip and he slapped me.

"You don't touch me again!" I screamed.

"I will do what I want! You were given to me!"

He shoved me against the tree in the middle of the garden and pressed his hand between my legs. I clenched my thighs around his arm and kicked him in his shin and ran toward the far east edge of the garden. He howled, an animal. I heard branches cracking under his feet as he chased me. Panther leapt from the tree in the middle of the garden and roared. Adam screamed and I just kept running. Sweat poured into my eyes. My heels thumped the grass. Lightning snapped across the sky and I saw panther running beside me toward the desert at the edge of the garden. The thunder came a few seconds later, then more lightning and then the downpour. A freezing, pelting rain carried me to the end of the garden. Panther jumped over the hedges and looked back at me. I hesitated only a moment before I climbed onto the safety of her back. Adam stayed behind in the garden alone.

It was a few months before I knew what stories he had told. The story of Snake. The apple. Me and the fall of mankind. I know what has happened to this world as a result of my moment of freedom. But I would still make the same choice. I would listen to my heartbeat, and I would feel the movement in my womb, and I would claim my freedom again. Without it, I would have died.

Now, I give it back to you.

Live.

In the Beginning

$\mathcal{D}$eep in the center of the center of the center of my center, Maya sleeps. Maya, Great Creatress, full belly rising and falling with each breath. She breathes the slow breath of sleep — the labored breath of one who has been tortured, raped, imprisoned and burned — the soft, releasing breath of mother surrendering her spirit so that her child might live — the resigned breathing of one who has been told "no" more times than she has been held or comforted or listened to — the short, staccato breath of one who buried son after son after son — the waxy, filtered breath of one who has not spoken her truth. Her breasts, round and heavy, fall to her sides beside her thick arms, nipples slowly dripping fluid down her flesh.

The center of the center of the center of my center is filled with sand — the soft kind — the kind that shapes itself into spirals and moats and castles where there are dragons and fairies and magic. The soft sand collects itself and presses itself snug against Maya's sleeping body. Each breath makes her body heavier. Each breath presses her deeper into the sand, into the earth, into my center.

The ocean, black, and deep and full of life, crashes onto the sand, caking it into thick bricks where sand crabs scurry and leave tiny tracks back to the sea. The ocean spits and rumbles, her waters reflecting yellow back to Grandmother Moon. Maya's breathing resonates with the ebb and flow of the waves.

I have to lie next to her to hear her heartbeat pulsing softly between her breasts. If I lie still and rest my ear over her heart, I find my own breath changing, synchronizing with hers. I find my own heartbeat slowing to a gentle thump-thump, thump-thump that also beats warm and constant in my temples and my wrists. The salt spray coats us both in cool, sticky film. Her flesh is thick and dark as the new moon. I am pale skinned, and my flesh is soft and new.

As I relax my weight onto hers, I feel my bones dissolving into feathers beating against the walls of my skin. My eyes close, but my soul opens and I hear the life sounds of the ocean swimming through me. I hear the whale songs and I hear their crying. I feel Maya's arms wrap around me and for an instant I am paralyzed. I hold my breath and my heart beats faster. I blink open my eyes and find she is also awake, her massive brown eyes filled to overflowing with salt water.

She knows me with her touch, with the rising and falling of her chest and with the flowing of her blood with the crossing of the moon. I stare at her open eyes, aware yet unaware, of the magnificence of her.

Maya shifts in her bed of sand and the world tilts. She stretches one arm and then the other and the seagulls come to life, splashing their wings through the air. She wiggles her toes and the creatures of the earth, the worms and snakes and spiders, start to breathe. She sits up and brushes the sand off her shoulders with huge and mighty hands, and with each swipe of her arm the landlocked creatures appear — the cats and wolves and monkeys.

I hold tight to her neck and kiss the soft and sturdy flesh of her earlobe. She sneezes and I hold even tighter as the fish and dolphins and snails appear. But when she stands tall, tall as any mountain I have ever seen, she drips blood red milk onto the sand and blesses the earth and creates woman.

Woman...Creatress...Giver of Life...Guardian of the Creatures. The new woman smiles at me from the sand and I curl up closer with Maya, wrapping my legs around her neck, hanging on to her shoulders, my face pressing between her breasts, breathing deep the smell of life.

Maya walks tall toward the ocean, her dark flesh jiggling with each step. I cling so tight I think my fingers will break. I cling to her, my mother. As we step into the sea, the waves part for us and Maya smiles. She places me on the foaming crest of a wave and as I float she says,

"Daughter, you are blessed and beautiful and good. You are free. Let no one own you or tame you. Follow your heart and trust in your intuition, for it comes from me. You are a child of mine, made in my image, and I am most pleased."

And she kisses me and releases me and I take with me her heartbeat and her moonblood and her courage as I swim into the salty night a woman.

The People vs. Judas Iscariot

$\mathcal{J}$udas Iscariot crushed his home grown cigarette out on the edge of the table. "Yo, listen up. It didn't really happen like they tell you. Man, don't you know not to believe everything you read? Look around you, baby. How was I supposed to know you all was gonna react like this? You'd think there wasn't justice before *People's Court.*" He shifted in his chair, crossing a thin right leg over the left. "So, man, what brings you by?"

I cleared my throat. I didn't know what to say. I thought this whole case was a practical joke. The D.A. himself could hardly keep from laughing when he gave me the assignment. He swore it was the real deal. And there he is. Judas. *The* Judas. I wondered if he was a war Vet. Judas coughed.

"I'm David Goldburg. The state has assigned me to represent you." I held out my hand. He was dark with a thick black beard that had long ago passed its optimum length. He focused his brown eyes on me and I withdrew my hand, wiping it awk-

123

wardly on my gray suit pants. "You — um — want to begin by telling me what happened?" I shifted in my chair. This man doesn't blink.

He lit another cigarette — his third since I'd started counting. "Get out," he whispered.

"Pardon me?"

"Get out. I don't need counsel."

"Mr. Iscariot, I'm not sure you understand the gravity of the charges." I gnawed on my gold-plated Cross pen. I had to keep this case. This could make my career, not to mention all the networks for the play by play. "Maybe I'll leave you alone for awhile and you can rethink your situation."

"Mr. Goldburg." He exhaled thick black smoke. "Ain't no position to rethink." He stood up — a powerful figure. Muscular chest and legs and exceptionally tall — about six foot nine or so. Even wearing dirty robes and worn, tan sandals he was awesome. I inadvertently sucked my breath sharply between my teeth. His hair was tied back in a ponytail and I noticed a tiny Star of David glistening in his right ear.

"I'm afraid there is. You see, he wants to press charges."

"He who?"

"You know who! Jesus H. Christ, that's who."

"He never told me he had a middle name." Judas ground his cigarette out on the table. "Sure this guy ain't a fake?"

His voice was so soft and gentle. It rubbed raw against his tone. He couldn't possibly be a traitor. Someone down at the D.A.'s office must have made a mistake. "You know what I mean."

"Yeah," he paused and tapped my notebook lightly with his knuckles. "You wanna open that and take notes? I'll tell you what happened that night." I opened my book and wiped my saliva from my tortured pen. "You might not want to know the

124   *Monsoons*

story. Could change a lot of lives." I was hooked. I saw myself chatting about this night with Barbara Walters. "Now this is all off the record."

"Absolutely."

"Jesus Christ, Mr. Christ, don't wanna press no charges."

"I beg to differ. You see, he filed with the D.A. this morning and — "

"No choice."

"I'm sorry?"

"He had no choice. Didn't leave me one neither. We both had no choice."

Where the hell was my tape recorder? No one would believe this conversation took place. I didn't believe it myself. But that didn't mean the tabloids wouldn't. "What do you mean, 'No choice?'" I straightened in my seat, pen poised above the paper.

"We're all pawns." He patted his left breast pocket but there were no more cigarettes.

How many times had I heard this angle? It wasn't my fault. I'm a black kid in the ghetto. It wasn't my fault. My father sexually assaulted me from the time I was four. It wasn't my fault. I'm on welfare. After awhile the excuses became as meaningful as Nixon's inauguration speech.

"You don't know what to make of me, do you?" he asked.

I have no idea what I said. I just remember my tongue itched.

"I need another smoke, man," he said.

"I don't smoke."

Judas looked squarely at me.

"I'll be right back," I muttered, and left the holding cell to look for a cigarette machine. When I returned with a half empty pack of Camels I'd found on a coffee table, he was standing in the corner facing the wall. "Sorry. This was all I could find."

Judas took three large steps and stood in front of me. He nodded. "That's cool, man. Thanks." He pulled out a smoke and lit a match from the leg of the table. His eyes closed as he exhaled, his lips parting slightly to release the smoke. "He came to me."

"Beg your pardon?"

"Jesus came to me. He needed my services for his whole deal to go down, you know? I was working late at the garage one night — real late — must have been after midnight 'cause the TV had signed off and I'd just cut on the radio. There's this great late night blues show I love. Anyway, I had just rolled back under the car when I hear this amazingly deep voice. Freaked me out, you know? I thought I was alone. It was the middle of the night and that garage ain't exactly Fort Knox.

"This guy reached for my ankle and started pullin' on it, draggin' me out from under the car. Well, I reached for my piece 'cause I was sure this was it. I'd had some dealings with some pretty rotten punks, if you know what I mean. I screamed at him. 'Let go of my fuckin' leg!' But he wouldn't, so I said, 'I've got a gun, man. I swear I'll shoot your ass off!' But the dude wouldn't let go so I had to fire. I thought for sure I nailed him, but he didn't let go. Didn't scream or anything. That's when I really freaked. You know these guys that are on that heavy duty shit can't feel any pain. 'I shot you, man! I shot you!' I shouted, but he kept pullin' on me 'til I could see his whole body. I'm tellin' ya, he was the scariest dude I'd ever seen." Judas slowly licked his lips. I noticed they were chapped. "Muddy Waters was on the box."

"This guy looked down at me and he was black as a swamp and his hair was thick and long. Looked like a mane all around his shoulders. I smelled this foo-foo odor. Like incense or something. Probably to cover up the fact that he ain't had a shower in weeks. I could see the clumped dirt, lighter than his skin, on his legs. But his voice was soft. Didn't fit. What's the word? A dichotomy?

"He looked right at me and said, 'I need you, Judas.' Thought I was gonna cream my shorts right then.

"'Pardon me?' I said.

"'I need you, Judas. Stand up and follow me.'

"Man, I don't know about you, but when some big black motherfucker shows up in the middle of the night not afraid of no gun and says follow me, I say hey, whatever you say."

Judas paused and looked at me. His eyes were empty. "You a Jew?"

"Goldburg." I fiddled with my pen. Always ashamed of that.

"Yeah. That's what I thought."

"Am I wrong?" I blurted out.

"Wrong? No man, you ain't wrong. Ain't exactly right, though."

"Well, who's right? Christians aren't right are they?"

He let out a deep, rich laugh. "I wouldn't worry too much about that." He stretched his legs out straight in front of him, letting his sandals fall to the floor. The gray cement walls seemed to pull towards each other, shrinking our space. There was one table and three chairs and no window, just the two-way glass that took up the entire north wall. He didn't seem aware of his surroundings. I turned over a clean page in my notebook. "Want to hear the rest?" he said.

I nodded.

"OK. This guy holds out his hand to help me up.

"'I'm Jesus,' he said.

Laraine Herring   127

"'Right, and I'm Tinkerbell.' I said.

"I wouldn't take his hand. I stood up on my own, although I thought about getting even and rubbing grease on him. So dark and dirty he probably wouldn't notice.

"'Leave your things and follow me.' he said.

"I don't mind telling you, I'd had enough of this jerk by this time. 'Look man,' I said. 'I don't know who you are, but I sure as hell know you ain't Jesus, and even if you were I sure as hell ain't following you. I got me a woman and a home and she'll bite my cock off if I don't show up soon.'

"Jesus crossed to the office and rolled out my desk chair. 'Sit,' he said. 'My father and I need you.'

"I was really starting to reach pure terror here. 'I'm going to call the police,' I said. And then, well this is when I guess it happened."

Judas' voice trailed off and I looked up from my notes. He was staring straight ahead, unblinking, fiddling with his earring. "Mr. Iscariot?" I said.

"Hmmm — huh?" He drifted back to me. "Sorry. Where was I?"

"You were about to call the police." I tapped my pen on the table. This man is certifiable.

"Oh yeah. Well, when I went to use the phone this dude started to glow. No foolin'. I swear on my mother he did. I'm clean too. I know what you're thinking. I ain't done drugs in years. I admit, I thought, damn, this is one hell of a flashback. This dude swallowed way too much kryptonite. But once the glowing thing started I just sat my ass back down and hoped that maybe if I kept my mouth shut he'd go away and haunt somebody else's garage.

"'Come with me,' he said and this time I figured, what the hell, and we walked outside where there was this gang of people waiting. I thought for sure this was somebody's initiation test and I was about to be sacrificed. Jesus had stopped glowing and blended right into the night. I could only see his eyes and his fingernails.

"'Who's that?' some guy standing under a streetlight asked.

"'This is Judas,' Jesus said. 'Judas, these are the disciples. Matt's in the car, here's John and Peter and James. This is James Two and that one's Thomas and there's Andy and Bart and Simon and Phil and here's another Judas. He's just James' kid. Kinda tagging along for now.'

"I nodded. I tell you, this was major de ja vu. They all piled into this stretch limo that was waiting just around the corner. 'Follow me,' he said again. I think this dude only knew a few words. His accent was kinda heavy and I could tell he wasn't from around here. Not even the east side. We all piled into this car and god in heaven, it was sweet! Like a limo for Elvis, you know? Jesus passed around beer for everybody — Lite — and then he looked straight at me and it was like everyone else in the car just disappeared.

"'I'm only going to say this once,' he said.

"'Look man,' I said. 'I don't know what I did to you guys, but whatever it was I didn't mean it. I don't have any money but you can have my car. It's a great car. Brand new. Not even five thousand miles on it yet.'

"Then he touched my lips with his index finger and I couldn't open my mouth. My tongue wagged around behind my teeth, but I couldn't utter a sound.

"'Do you know who I am?' he asked.

"'You say you're Jesus,' I said. He could be whoever the hell he wanted as long as he let me out of the damn car.

"'I am Jesus. Look at me. Look at my eyes. Do you know

Laraine Herring   *129*

who I am?'

"I looked straight into his eyes although I was scared shitless. It was like they opened up into two giant big screen TV's and I saw the most amazing things. I saw myself when I was a kid shootin' hoops at school, then I saw my father shooting himself behind some building and after that I saw Ted Bundy and Jim Jones and Ghenghis Khan and then I saw this fine woman. She had dark olive skin and emerald eyes and the longest black hair I'd ever seen.

"'That's my mother,' he said softly.

"'Hey, man, I didn't mean nothin'!' I said quickly. The woman shone deep in his eyes. I could only guess at her shape, but I was looking at her soul. She was so pure Jesus couldn't keep her behind his eyes and she shot out at me like a laser.

"'You must help my son,' she said, and then we were in darkness again. I don't mind telling you I was shaking so hard my teeth were chattering practically off my gums.

"'Man, what you takin'?' I asked Jesus. Someone kicked me in the leg. I thought it was Phil.

"'Yo,' he said. 'We'll take you back right after the gig.' Then he softened. 'Don't be afraid. We're all in the same boat.'

"'Here.' Jesus said and the driver stopped. 'They're waiting for me.' His voice was silky, a young James Earl Jones. He covered my hands with his and looked me straight in the eyes. 'I'm going up that hill.' He pointed north to the Peak. Spooky. 'They're just over there beyond that fence. As soon as I'm out of sight, go tell them you know where I am.'

"'Look man,' I said. 'I ain't getting involved in the middle of a damn gang war. Think I don't see what's goin' down? I tell them where you are, they come after you, you kill me because I ratted you out. I don't think so. Find another sucker.'

"'There is no one else,' he said, and I swear he was kinda

sad. I thought he felt almost sorry for yanking me out of my garage in the middle of the night. Come to think of it, I ain't never seen a man look more alone. He climbed out of the limo and motioned for me to get out too. As soon as I closed the door, the car sped away.

"'They just gonna leave you like that? Man, I'd get me some new disciples. Your brothers ain't supposed to leave you like that!'

"'They'll be back.' He didn't seem worried.

"'But hey, what if these other dudes have machine guns or something?' I was getting hysterical.

"'These other — dudes —' said Jesus 'are going to kill me.'

"'Is this Candid Camera? I thought Candid Camera went off the air. Just let me go home, man, and I swear I'll say I never saw you.'

"I heard a loud noise behind us and I expected any minute to see the troops marching out of the night like at Normandy.

"'It's almost time,' he said.

"'Man, we don't have to do this!' I screamed. Suddenly, I wanted desperately to protect this man. I kept seein' his Mama, and well, everybody's got a mama. Sure, he was a little wacked out, but I didn't think he'd ever hurt anybody.

"'I do have to die,' he said. 'And you have to turn me in. I'm sorry. It's your destiny. Believe me, you weren't my first choice.'

"'Fuck destiny! What do you mean I wasn't your first choice?'

"'I wanted Whoopi Goldberg. We got close after *Ghost*. Just kidding. Relax. Your destiny is to go into that field and tell them where I am. Then get out of town. You can take your wife, but leave your car so it looks like you could have been killed.' Jesus placed both his hands on my shoulders. It was almost like a hug, so I jerked away from him. I wasn't into that shit. 'Listen, Judas, people are going to say all kinds of things about you. They're going to look for you and want to kill you. You need to know that I know and my father knows that you had no choice.' He handed me a light brown paper sack. By the time I looked inside and saw the wad of green, he'd vanished. Man, I'm fucked. That's all I could think. I'm fucked. I'm fucked. I'm fucked."

Judas was silent for about five minutes. I thought he was waiting for me to catch up. "Excuse me?" I said softly when I'd finished writing the last sentence. "Is that it?"

"Is that it?" He was stunned.

"Then why is he pressing charges? Why isn't he dead?"

"The L.A.P.D. interfered and screwed everything up."

I bristled. "To their credit, they were trying to avert a gang war."

"They won't avert this. He needs me again for another night. That's why I don't need counsel. Let them set bail, he'll pay it and this damn cycle can start all over again."

"Cycle?"

"Life is a circle, Mr. Goldburg. A man can't change his fate. Trust me. I tried." He stubbed out his last cigarette from the pack I'd found for him. A loud knock startled me, but Judas didn't even flinch. "Nope. Can't escape God."

"An anonymous party posted bail for Mr. Iscariot," said the officer at the door. "He's free to go."

"Thanks for the smokes, counselor." Judas smiled quickly, touched my shoulder and walked out the door into the lobby of the Orange County Police Station.

I closed my notebook, snapped shut my briefcase and

stared at my reflection in the two-way window.

Can't escape God. I noticed something shiny on the table. His Star of David earring. He must have taken it off and I just didn't notice. Great observation skills, Goldburg.

I picked it up. I was surprised that the delicate shape of the earring felt quite substantial between my fingers. I quickly slipped it in my pocket, lit one of the half burned cigarettes Judas had consumed in the last few hours, placed it to my lips, inhaled deeply and closed my eyes, trying to exhale the envy through my nose.

Light Of The World

$\mathcal{T}$he wind howled across the desert, flattening Mary's hair against her face. She laughed, brushed it away with one hand, and reached for Jesus who sat next to her on the rock, watching the dust devils in the distance.

"What do you see?" she asked.

"All kinds of things," he whispered, turning to her. "Hear the wind? It's crying."

"You always talk in pictures. You're the only man I know who talks in pictures all the time."

"That's how I see," said Jesus. "Everywhere I look I see pictures. I hear things. Ghosts. Whispers of events. Images. The things I see, Mary." He reached for her hand. "I'm so glad you're here."

"I remember watching you as a boy." Her palm tingled where he touched her, and she remembered the first time he had come to her. He was a young man, fourteen, she thought.

He had peeked into her tent and seen the men waiting in the sweltering heat to buy a piece of her flesh. He waited until the last man had gone home to his wife before he finally approached her. She'd been lying on her mat, nude, with just a silk cloth covering her legs. Her hair was matted to her head, and she smelled of others' sweat.

"Hello?"

"I'm closed. Come back tomorrow." Mary stretched her arms above her head and repositioned herself so she could catch a hint of the breeze. She saw the young boy and pulled the scarf over her breasts. "Son, run along to your mama."

He came inside anyway and sat, lotus position, beside her on the ground. "You're beautiful," he said after a long while.

"I'm a whore."

"No, you're not. You're a beautiful woman."

She laughed. Her voice was hoarse. "And what do you know about beautiful women? You're barely old enough to fetch the water from the well."

He didn't smile. He looked at her, slowly lingering on her eyes and mouth. Finally, he spoke. "What were those men waiting for?"

"Get on out of here and go home." Her eyes watered. "Get on out of here."

"What were those men waiting for?"

She twisted her long black hair between her fingers. "They were waiting for me."

"Why?"

"Why?" The skin on Mary's neck prickled. She threw her pillow at him. He didn't move. He just reached his arms out in front of him to catch it.

"Yes, Mary. Why?"

"Fine. I'll say it. They buy me. Me. My body. My pussy.

My tits. My ass. Me. My flesh. Happy?"

"Are you?"

"Who are you?"

"My name is Jesus. I think you're beautiful."

Mary laughed. "Come here, kid. You want one for free? You just got it." She patted the warm place beside her.

"No. I just want to touch you. If that's OK." He shifted on the mat, his robes falling over his legs.

"Sure honey." She lifted the silk cloth and revealed her thighs, her stomach, her vagina.

"No, not there." He covered her with the cloth and reached for her face. "Here." And with the back of his hand, he stroked her cheek, under her chin, around her ear. He ran his fingers through her raven hair, stopping at each tangle to untwist the hairs, spreading it smooth over her bare shoulders. Mary's heart pounded. Her flesh burned. Her lips parted and she sighed.

"Who are you?"

"I came to be your friend."

"Honey, I don't have friends," she said softly. But she gasped and squeezed her thighs.

"Yes, you do," he said, and lay beside her on the mat, feeling the desert wind over his body.

Mary snuggled closer to Jesus as the wind picked up. "You were fascinating to me," said Jesus. "I used to watch you at the well from my tent. You always held your head up. That's what I noticed."

She took his face between her hands and tucked a stray piece of hair behind his ear. "You, my friend, were the only one who ever talked to me."

"That's such a shame. I will always talk to you."

"Yes." She brought his lips to hers and brushed them with her tongue. She giggled. "You taste good."

He wrapped his arms around her and pulled her close. "Not as good as you," he whispered.

She took his tongue and wrapped hers around it and sucked it into her mouth. He ran his fingers over her shoulders, reached down her robe and cupped her breasts. She moaned. "Here? Outside?"

He smiled. "Why not? There's no one around. You'll be safe with me."

"I'm always safe with you." She lay back onto the rock. "I'm so grateful you came to me."

Ravens circled above them. Mary thought she could feel the breeze from their flapping wings.

"It's you I am grateful for," said Jesus. "I couldn't do this without you. You are my rock." He kissed her deeply, felt her nipples harden against his flesh. "You are my love," He breathed her in.

"Don't think about it. Not now. Not here. Just be here with me now."

He lifted her arms above her head and slid her robe over them. She shivered warmly as the silk caressed her skin. "I am here now, Mary. How can I not think of it? I think of it all the time. I am afraid."

"Shhh. Don't be afraid. I will be with you always, even unto the end."

Jesus took her breasts in his hands and caressed her nipples gently. She arched her back. "I know. You and my mother. You are the two who will be with me always. I know."

"Don't talk. That day will come soon enough. Today we have the desert and the ravens and the sky. Look at the beautiful sky. We have each other. We have this moment. That is enough."

"It's not enough." He slid his robes over his shoulders and lay on top of her. She felt him harden against her thigh.

"It has to be enough, my love. It has to be."

Mary reached for him and pulled him down between her legs. She felt his sadness through his tongue — his desperate, probing tongue. She knew this was the last night. She knew tomorrow his worst fears would come true. Tomorrow they would come for him. Late at night. A night that smelled like this, perhaps, of wine and sandalwood and jasmine. Damp and living. One of his men would turn on him. One of the ones he trusted. But history would write her differently. She arched into him, quivering.

"Yes, Mary," he smiled, lifted his head, his lips shimmering in the light.

"Kiss me."

He leaned down and kissed her and she drank him in. "I don't want to stop," he whispered.

"Then don't."

The sun set behind the mountains. Let it last, she thought. Please, let it last.

She spread her legs wide and Jesus entered her, filling her. She screamed and clutched his back, digging in her nails. She wrapped her legs around his neck, pulling him in deeper. With each thrust, she saw a vision. The first vision was red and black, with thorns and screaming screeching ravens. The next vision was wet, rain and tears streaking down wood, lightning cracking through a black black sky. The third vision was quicker, searing yellow light, red bleeding into yellow turning pink, turning green turning black. The fourth vision appeared as she arched her back, and stomach to stomach, they came and she became raven flying through the sky, carrying his spirit on her back.

He collapsed onto her, breathing deeply, beads of sweat dotting his forehead. She stroked his long black hair, kissed his brown skin, breathed deep the smell of his flesh, imprinting it on her heart.

"Mary, I —"

"Shhh. I know. You don't have to say anything. I know."

His body shook against hers. She looked at the stars as his tears splashed her shoulder. "It'll be tomorrow."

"I know."

"Where will you be?"

"Beside you. As always."

He sat up and she wrapped him in her cloak. He held her close and she leaned her head against his arm.

"It's beautiful out here."

"Yeah," he said. "Look out over there. See the mountains? The silhouette? It looks like a cat, don't you think?"

"A cat?" She laughed. "You've been out in the desert too long."

"No really. See?"

She squinted her eyes in the moonlight. She saw two ears, and if she closed one eye and cocked her head she could see two haunches and maybe the hint of a tail. "OK. I see it, love."

"Tomorrow they'll come."

She took his hand and squeezed it. "I'll be here."

"We could take off tonight. Go to the desert. Maybe head out to India. China."

"Baby, you've been to India and China. Your place is here now."

He looked into the dark canyon. She couldn't see his eyes, only the dark streaks on his face. He bowed his head. Mary pulled him toward her, stroking his hair. "You'll be here?"

She nodded, her long hair covering him like a shawl. She covered his neck with kisses. "I have always loved you," she said.

"And I you." He playfully bit her neck. "You are the light of my world."

"I am your friend."

He touched her cheek. "My friend."

"You are the love of my life."

He looked deep in her eyes and she saw the fear, the love and the horror in his heart. "You will move on."

"As will you, Jesus. As will you."

He nodded and brushed his lips lightly against hers, lingering as long as he could. They separated slowly, their lips peeling apart like ripe fruit. Jesus and Mary sat side by side and wept and watched the stars shift while they held hands and listened for the soldiers' footsteps on the rocks below.

Virgin Evening

$\mathcal{S}$he had pledged her eternal love to Jesus Christ, the only Son of our Lord, when she was 14. She'd slid the thin gold band on her ring finger and promised fidelity and honesty until death. Now she sat on her cot, smoothed her dress around her shackled ankles, and tried to peer out the tiny window that was on the far north wall of her cell. She had no mirror, so she had felt her face for the past few days, trying to find the familiar lines, hoping not to find any new ones, her fingers traveling the crevasses by her nose, her lips, her eyes, resting at the base of her neck, pressing firmly against her jugular.

"Thou shalt not kill."

Sweet Jesus, now at 33, she was alone. Nights of making love to her invisible savior vanished into memories, dreams, visions, then only ideas, only a thought, a plan, a possibility. Like the sounds of the ocean in a conch shell, she remembered her fingers pressed firm on her thighs, sliding slippery inside her, her body electric and open to herself.

Today they planned to kill her. Her sacred sisters had abandoned her once they found out what she had done. So clear cut to them, she thought. Life makes so much sense to them in their moss-covered stone chapels, beautiful gardens, safe solitude. One way to God. One path for redemption.

The man had come to her one night when there was no moon. He must have snuck in under the cover of darkness, the cloak of silence always present at the convent after the dinner hour. He could have been sent by Satan to test her, but she didn't believe in Satan. Didn't believe in the church's ideas of God's plans and tests for his children. She believed that Jesus would comfort her, be kind to her, hold her long into the night, touching her hair softly like he had stroked Mary Magdalene's so many centuries ago.

Women were freer then. This was the Middle Ages, only no one had yet named it. It was simply the present time and certain things were immutable, certain things were permanent. Many things were evil. She was now evil. She, who had fled to the wide open embrace of the Church for salvation, for sanctity, for security. She, who had no home, no place, no hearth, because a woman without a man was a nomad. A constant traveller in circles until some male force took pity on her and held her close.

Jesus had come to her in a dream and told her he had a place waiting for her in his Kingdom. She had nowhere else to go, so when she held out her hand to the Christ and when she pressed his wounded palm against her chest, she cried because he only wanted to heal her. He didn't want to pinch or poke or prod or suck the outer edges of her body. So she said yes to Him, body and soul, and found a home. His thick brown hair would cover her chest and belly as they slept, spoon position,

Monsoons

not dreaming. She held his promises deep in the dark part of her heart.

She could only believe the man had gotten in after dinner, when they were all in the chapel whispering evening vespers. She did not know why he chose her room, her body, her soul. She had felt his hands, hot in a different way than her own, than her Lord's. Then she felt something thick and foreign pushing into her and she screamed, locked her fingers around his neck, and shook him off, discarding his carcass on the stone floor like dishwater. People came running, more people than she had ever seen, poking at the body, poking at her, binding her hands and taking her away. The good sisters prayed for her, she knew this, but they couldn't, wouldn't, defend her.

She had killed a man. She had murdered for the honor of Christ, her husband, but rules were different for women. Women could not refuse. Women could not defend their honor. That was an honor reserved for men, soldiers, judges; for God. She heard the rich deep tones of the bell ringing in the square. Soon there would be loud footsteps in the hallway and the guards would enter her cell, this time with a priest, and ask her once again if she repented what she'd done. She would look straight ahead until they blindfolded her and she would twist the thin gold band on her ring finger and for the first time wonder if Jesus would indeed be waiting for her, arms outstretched, food on the stove, warm blanket on the bed, when she pushed against the wrought iron gates of heaven and proclaimed,

"Husband? I'm home."

Zanna (a monologue)

$\mathcal{I}$'m the kid who you looked at growing up and thought had everything in the world. You were jealous of me, each of you in your own way. Maybe you didn't even realize it. But I did. I knew by the way you looked at me and the way you stopped talking when I walked past you in the halls. I could tell by the way I somehow managed to live somewhat intimately with most of you for twenty years and not one of you had the courage to be my friend. Not one of you were willing to make a decision that went against your parents or your preacher. I spent years sitting next to you in algebra, running with you on the track, or singing with you in the school musical, but would you ever take the time to get to know me? No. All you could do was titter and make your little jokes and speculate and torture torture torture.

Well, I'll tell you one thing. Thank you. You made me who I am. Not the money, not the fancy schools, not the very best efforts of the good Christian women of Mississippi. You and your scorn made me a fighter. And that's what I have to be. That's what I was born to be.

I'm older than any of you. Always have been. You can chronicle age in more than years, you know. I suppose I should take you back a bit. So you know who I am, where I come from, how I got to be the way I am now. I was born in Biloxi, Mississippi, which is handicap enough if you've got any brain at all. My family is a wonderful old Southern family (massa's in the slave house again) with wonderful old money that was acquired through better-than-average land management during the Reconstruction and enough fortitude to recognize that the "free Negroes" still needed to work and so for slightly more than nothing, great great grandpa Franklin would reacquire all his free Negroes and continue to operate his cotton fields. To this day, we have descendants from those "reacquired" Negroes working for us. To ask daddy about it, he'd swear they were family. Well, once I was in high school I dated one of "them", mostly out of curiosity, and I soon learned they were not family.

The year is 1965. I am a flower child. Only my parents wore three piece suits and sensible shoes. My parents sang in the choir and never questioned. My parents were a rock to my brother and me, a solid foundation for him, a crushing mass of hypocrisy for me. I wore white Easter dresses with black patent leather shoes and bobby socks. I wore cute little bows in my hair and had the most beautifully furnished doll house of anyone in my class. My plan was simple as a little girl. I wanted to take over the world. I mellowed slightly as I aged, but only slightly.

Laraine Herring 145

There were two schools of thought in 1965. Left and right, pro and con. Doesn't take a rocket scientist to figure out I came from the right. There was one answer and one answer only in my house. It is God's will. Whatever "it" might be. We had a wide oak staircase that you could see when you walked through the front door. On the white walls going up to the second floor were pictures. My great grandfather, my grandfather, and, the largest and in color, my father. They watched us, a stream of men, dead eyes prying into all manners of our business. They watched us sneak up the stairs if we came in too late and watched our good-bye kisses through the window when we might be standing there with a new friend. They watched the family holidays and they watched the family fights. They were included in the prayers and a place was saved for them at church.

Literally, we were ruled by the dead. We lived with the dead. It's of little surprise to me that I became haunted by the dead. But I wasn't haunted by the eyes of the photos. I was haunted by the women who knew the eyes of the photos. No one ever spoke of them. No one ever mentioned grandma except to comment on how much she loved grandad and how she was never the same after he died. Everyone told me she went a little batty. Batty is Southern for different. Funny, because the one thing I was told about grandma was that she dyed her thinning hair red and started wearing genie pants and beads. She took up the harmonica and the neighbors would often comment that they could hear her playing from her porch until the early morning hours. She took her privacy very seriously all of a sudden, and she dropped out of the ladies circle at the church. Folks were concerned. Folks were downright worried. They say she died lying on her crocheted bedspread, sun washing across her face, a wide smile splashed across her lips. I'm sure that's how it happened, too. Because she's never spoken of except in hushed tones late at night that sound so much like wind through the oleanders that you're not even sure you heard anything at all. But I know I heard them. And once I accepted what I heard and welcomed her into my heart, her spirit, her batty spirit, began haunting me.

Grandma doesn't come just at night either. She's about taken up permanent residence with me. It's OK. I call her Rosa. Even though her name was Louise. Her ghost name is Rosa. Gives me a lot of insight into who she is. A name, a real, honest chosen name, tells us everything we ever need to know about a woman. Know her name and know her hands. My given name is Hosanna Mae Franklin, but only my family calls me Hosanna. I chose Zanna early on. Sometimes people call me Z, but I like Zanna. I love Zanna, actually. She's me. Many things about me didn't fit in, right from the start. I picked myself up when I was two and started walking. Never crawled. No time for it. I pierced my nose too. Now this is years and years before anyone did. Took a collective twenty years off my parents' lives I'm sure. They made me take it out of course, but ironically, the hole never closed up, and as soon as I was eighteen I put my diamond stud back in it.

I was too smart and I could play ball, and if that's not official geek makings than I don't know what is. I played all kinds of sports and I was usually better than the boys. Basketball was my favorite. Running up and down the court, tennis shoes squeaking on the floor, sweat dripping in my eyes, down my back, running and running and running as fast as I could until it felt like my legs were merging with the court, one living breathing organism, pushing me closer and closer to the basket. The ball leaves my hands and I see the net, almost opening wider for the ball, then swish! YES! The roar of the crowd, the slaps from my teammates, the complete total orgasmic satisfaction that comes from a slam dunk. The speed, sweat, and skill. I loved it.

You can imagine I was never encouraged. Mom wanted me to sing in the choir or help with the nursery or do any number of things I had no intention of doing. I ripped up my choir robe and turned it into a Batman cape. I thought that would have cured my mother of her choir dream, but instead she made me wear it during Sunday services. I think she thought I would be embarrassed, but I wasn't. I was proud, and I can envision how I must have looked, rebellious daughter of the choir director, mouthing the words to "Jacob's Ladder" in a batcape. I'm sure mother was the one mortified, but she never said a word. She didn't say many words to me, actually. She crammed Jesus down my throat like medicine. She told me that He loved me, but only if I changed who I was. God made me, but he didn't intend for me to be who I am. I should be like Jesus, and in so many ways I am like Jesus, but these are ways my mother will never understand. Her life is black and white, and it's taken her the better part of it to construct an environment where she can function. I have been angry at her for many years. Now I'm sad for her. Her heart is just not big enough. I would like to know more about her. I would like to know why she can claim Christ as her personal savior and not be able to love me. I think now that I've found some peace of my own, I still love her. How does a girl not love her mother? Somehow, it's easier to understand why she didn't love me.

I think I would have loved my grandmother Rosa. I would have loved the woman she became. All the women I admired growing up were not married. Batty. Women with husbands had families and families took something from you. It seemed a shame that I did not know one woman who could escape the bonds of family. Men, marriage, they take your name, they take your body, they take your life.

I never knew a partnership until I met women. A woman. An equal being. Suddenly my eyes were open like never before. My heart beat louder. I felt the rush like I'd felt playing basketball and I had no idea what to do. Things happen to me that I can't always explain. I've heard talk that we all choose our lives and I don't know as I would entirely disagree with that. I know I bring on drama. I want an exciting life and I want to matter. I buy books and write my name in them in flowing script — the "Z" long and flowery, flowing elegance. Then I write the date, because someone in the future will pick up the book and wonder who I am. Rosa speaks to me of these things. She tells me what life was like for her. She tries to tell me what life could be for me. Most of the time she teaches me to be confident. She speaks of sadness and loneliness and repression, but also of hope, and by contrast to her life she tries to tell me how great mine can be. She didn't expect to be a ghost. The afterlife didn't turn out like she'd expected either. I bet that happens to everyone. Human beings hate surprises. That's why we're so afraid to die. It's the biggest surprise of all.

People make me angry. Made me angry for a lot of years. Studying history made me angry. Learning about the cruelties done to men by men devastates me. It's because I can hear the screaming. I can't look at a picture of corpses in a mass grave or women in line for showers at Auschwitz and not feel hear the screaming. It's rather egotistical to assume that I can possibly feel the pain and devastation of the victims, but when I look at those photographs I see stories. I see families and bottom line is I see people, not nationalities, not religions, just people. People who for some unexplainable unimaginable reason have been dealt a cruel blow. How can we hope to make up for injustices like that?

I studied Latin for years. All our violent, warring words come from Latin. And through Latin I learned about men. I learned what men are capable of, by choice, and it frightened me. I wished I had studied Greek, or a softer language. Latin hardened me in a way I didn't want to admit I could be hardened. And Latin appealed to me in a base place in my soul where I didn't want to admit I could live. Much like watching a bloody car accident and hoping to catch a glimpse of a charred body, Latin and the language of war became addictive to me. I became hard at my center. That's about where I am now. Trying to figure out what I'm supposed to do with that hardness. Trying to figure out how to keep holding on to my battiness before the world takes it away from me. Trying to figure out how to be strong enough to let you love me. If you're up for it.

Air

*"Though the past haunts me as a spirit,
I do not ask to forget."*

- Felicia Hemans

In the House of the Lord

Harold's green eyes glowed in the dark like a wolf's the day he asked me to be his wife. Glowed like jealous coals in the dark swamp of his face. No emotion. They glinted at me and I saw a shadow of myself in their mirror. Me, in my bright blue Sunday hat with the red flowers on it. Me, in my best cream colored dress, the one that comes just above my knees. Me, so nervous my stockings were sticking to the backs of my legs. Me, who said yes to the farmer, who took his thick hand in hers and walked behind him into his life. Me, who still sits on the front porch with a tall glass of lemon water in the red plastic tumbler we bought at the Family Dollar Store and doesn't quite know what hit her.

Our house was at the end of about a mile and a half of dirt road, buried in part by oleanders, part by kudzu, with just enough creek in the backyard to make the humidity unbearable and the bugs active as the swamp frogs. Deep in August we never even got a breath of wind so low and so far back. I stood at my sink and blew at my lace curtains, now limp and yellow from dampness. Air was so thick and heavy I couldn't make them move. Time and again I swore I saw the air shimmering, rocking like waves, carrying the armies of bugs recklessly along like they were in wooden barrels going down Niagara Falls, unaware of their impending doom.

I tried to arrange my window shelf in my kitchen so I'd have something pretty to look at. I had to stand at that sink all day and wash those dishes and look out at the yard, at the land that should be "our" land, but really was Harold's land. My favorite possession was a piece of quartz that my granddaddy picked up on one of his treks along the Mississippi River. I set it on the shelf because I liked the way it shone when the sun touched it. Made me feel warm inside. I also liked to have a little tiny flowerpot of mint. Didn't take up all that much room really. Little tiny precious green leaves poking up from the dirt. Harold didn't like any of it.

"Clutter!" he'd say. "Why you always gotta be cluttering up the place with all this stuff that don't serve you a purpose except maybe for something else to dust." Then he'd storm out of the room and I wouldn't see him until morning. I'd usually find my quartz half stuck down the drain and my mint plant upside down in the backyard, all the little leaves crushed and trembling.

After Harold went out to the field, I took my quartz and shoved it deep in my apron pocket where I had to remember how it used to glisten. I gathered up my mint plant and tried to repot it, but it never seemed to take hold like before. I had to keep it in the spare room with all my sewing stuff. Harold never went in there and I figured I'd peek in on it, every now and then, and talk to it some. At least it would be alive, even if it didn't have a sunny windowsill.

While Harold was out working the marsh land, I stood in the sitting room in front of the mahogany mirror that used to belong to my Grannie. She'd carried it with her from the home of a white man on the last day she ever cleaned anybody else's dirt. I would smile at myself, admiring the rectangular gap between my front teeth. My face, especially around my mouth, glistened from sweat. I would spin around and run my hands across my ample backside, push up my breasts, lift my dress a little further above my knees. I would smile at myself in the privacy of the dark, hot parlor and think that I was indeed quite a woman. I would imagine that Harold still thought so and that maybe once when he came in from the field, he might want to stay one night with me, instead of rushing back off to town to find a paler girl with a smaller ass and bigger breasts; softer hair, a kinder tongue. I would imagine a faceless knight behind me in the mirror, holding out his hand to me, to dance with me, to walk with me. I wanted my knight's voice to sound like Harold's, but it never quite fit. My knight's voice was low and sure and soft as Peter Pan peanut butter. Harold's voice had become gruff and short and mean, when I heard it at all.

"Got to go easy on your man, child," my Mama tried to tell me when I was a girl. "He don't mean to hurt you. He just been put down and pushed around all day, he don't have nothing he can call his own except his house and his woman. It's important to a man to have something to be in control of. Just fate, I reckon, that says it's got to be us." My mama was too forgiving. She took the "turn the other cheek" verse way too personal. I watched my daddy beat her and degrade her and humiliate her until she could barely hold her head up. Then I knew he'd take her. And that's just what it would be. He would take her and when he was done with her he would leave.

No, sir. I swore I would not end up like my mama. I swore she was wrong. Maybe my daddy was like that, but it was a sickness of his own, not of the entire male population. I knew I wasn't destined for the same lot as mama, but somehow I found myself with Harold, the handsomest man in three counties, dancing with myself in front of an antique mirror, trying to believe my life hadn't really ended up in such a mess. Trying to find that fiery, quick tempered girl buried under the layers of fatty protection this woman-child had built all up around herself. Day after day I held onto that rock in my pocket, so tight sometimes my fingers stiffened up and I had to run hot water over them before I went to bed so I could relax enough not to dream.

"Do you promise to love, honor, and obey...until death do you part?" Reverend Marston looked up at me over metal-rimmed glasses. My mouth didn't waste a second, but my heart still hadn't gotten around to an answer.

"I do." I said, smiling widely at the Reverend, veiled face hidden mercifully from Harold. Harold squeezed my hand. This is what I am supposed to do. This is what life is. I could no more change my fate than I could make rain. I knew that. Harold knew that too, and he was happy. The way I saw it, after a year there were no more choices. Weeks melted into months, then years, the edges of each day blurring so much they simply became life. No more choices. Not my life. I was now a fixture in Harold's life. And what was worse, I had come willingly.

After our marriage ceremony and the unremarkable honeymoon at Island Motor Lodge, I began to wonder if a man's being the best looking guy in three counties was quite enough. It wasn't until I was well into my life that I began to think that I might have the right to ask for more.

One morning I woke up and sat on the chair by the vanity watching Harold sleep. He snored in spurts, and was all bundled up in the sheets he'd stolen from my side of the bed. His mouth was slightly open and a string of drool dripped down his cheek and onto the pillow. His fingers twitched like cat's ears and I could see the layers of dirt wedged so long under his fingernails that the nails had been stained brown. His hands were calloused, although I rarely felt them anymore except maybe on my shoulders or across my face. I thanked the good Lord that I could not have children. What would I do with a son and what could I do if I had a daughter?

I could see it, I'd be crouched on my knees in the kitchen scrubbing what was left of the pattern off the linoleum, and I'd try to tell her about men. I'd try to explain it to her and I'd turn into my mama. Wouldn't be able to help it. God forbid my girl-child might turn to me and ask me why they can't think about us for a change. Why we don't do something about it. What answer would possibly be good enough? None. I could say nothing. I would have to go back to my soapy water and my dingy floor and know that on that day I had finally sold my soul.

I found a tiny red bead in the garden one day, nestled around the stems of the zinnias. Looked like a little girl had lost her necklace back here years ago. The edge of the bead was cracked almost like it had been bitten. I put it in my apron pocket and I could hear it rubbing against the quartz, a symphony of two. When I got back to the house, I took the bead out and put it on the windowsill. The sun didn't shine through it like it had the quartz, but still it sat on the shelf, scarlet against the once bright white wood. I could look at it when I did the dishes and I could remember the moment I found it, precious as a ruby, buried in the dirt. Harold never noticed it either.

I think it was too small for him to see.

Sometimes, after Harold's gone off for the day, I sit in my rocker on the porch, drinking the last cup of coffee of the morning, and just dream. I let my eyes go flying up over the pine trees, down the long dirt driveway out to the center of town to the bus station. In my favorite fantasy a man would be at the depot standing under an umbrella even though it wasn't raining. He would notice me, look up from his paper and smile, ever so subtly. I would suddenly find it necessary to cross in front of the stranger and by chance drop my handbag. He would pick it up for me and subtly, again, ask me where I was headed. I would smile coquettishly, letting my gaze linger just a bit too long on his chest. He would offer to take me away to wherever I wanted. He was touring America on Greyhound and could use the company. That would be it then. I would be whisked away on a bus tour by a handsome stranger and I would never look back.

Oh, I know, that's not a very original fantasy. Not a very likely fantasy, either. I don't care. Usually something distracts me before I can get to any wondrous places. Some mosquito'll come along and get friendly with my arm or the phone will ring or maybe Anita from down the way will come calling. Doesn't take too long before I get too hot and my coffee gets too cold and I have to get up and go back inside and rejoin my life. Rejoin my dusting or scrubbing or polishing. Keeping surfaces clean. That's what I do. It doesn't matter what's crawling in the heating ducts or living down the drainpipe. What matters is the cabinet doors and front yard petunias. What matters is image. And I keep a Sunday-perfect image.

When Harold does come home, I never know for sure if he notices all I've done for him. All I've worked at to keep the neighbors impressed, keep his ego intact. Usually he notices the one weed I've left between the marigolds and the tulips, or the one speck of dirt on the coffee cup. At those times, I look at the floor and I wait for him to be quiet. Sometimes it's sooner than other times. Sometimes he carries on for days. I've learned not to listen. Sometimes the sounds of his rantings are comforting. I know he's home. I know he at least knows I'm at home, even though he acts like he'd prefer it if I'd just quietly get on out of his life some days.

A person can get used to a lot of things. Noise or quiet. It's all the same really. Whatever's habit. Habit is alright to deal with because it's consistent, and consistency's an unhappy woman's best friend. Oh, I hear you, mama. Yes, ma'am, I hear you.

So it was on a day like that, a day like any other day. I was on my porch, fanning a bug away from my eyes every now and then with an old sports page, thinking up over the pine trees to the bus station, thinking to the handsome stranger wanting company to Atlanta and beyond, when I heard whistling coming from the trees. It wasn't Wednesday, which was Anita's usual day for visiting, and it wasn't Saturday, which was the preacher's usual day for calling, so I stood up and rolled my newspaper into a paper bat and held it behind my back. The stranger emerged hat first from the woods still whistling. A beaten down yellow Lab padded along next to him. From where I stood, I thought the poor dog only had one and a half ears.

"Good morning, ma'am." He took off his straw hat and held it with both hands in front of his body.

"Good morning." Polite fellow.

"Can I interest you in some used treasures?" He burst

Laraine Herring   *159*

into a wide grin.

"Used treasures?"

"Junk, to the layman. Treasures to the trained, artistic eye. Which I can see from here, ma'am, you possess."

I involuntarily took a step backwards.

"I'm Clarence, ma'am. You don't need to be frightened of me. Old Clarence is perfectly harmless."

"What if I'm not?" He's looking me up and down, not totally sure what I meant by that. I could tell he's wrestling with himself, so I kept at it. "Aw, don't pay attention to me. I don't get much company down here. Sometimes I forget how to talk to anybody besides myself."

He sat down on the front porch steps. "Well, ma'am, if you don't mind my saying so, that's quite the shame."

I didn't mind him saying so at all, and squeezed myself down on the porch steps next to him. "So, Clarence," I said. "What all kind of treasures you got?"

Clarence's "used treasure" store was really nothing more than a handmade wooden cart with three thin wheels and a makeshift bed built onto the back for the dog. "No overhead," he said and smiled big and wide again. "Look at this." He pulled out a tarnished silver teapot with part of the handle chopped off. "Put some elbow grease to it and it'll be good as new."

"I don't know —" I already had a teapot.

"OK. I know. How about this?" He reached into his cart much deeper than I thought would have been possible. He pulled out a cup and saucer in perfect condition. "One of a kind! For you, ten dollars."

"No. That's the same pattern as my A&P dishes."

"Why, so it is!" He winked at me, amazed and amused

that he'd been caught. "I knew the minute I saw you that you were a collector of treasures too." He touched me just slightly on my arm, so briefly that it could have been accidentally in passing, but it reverberated off my flesh and through my body in an electric charge like I hadn't felt since fifth grade when Mama caught me touching myself in the dark under the covers.

"I've got the perfect thing." Clarence held out a long string of red beads, only a shade darker than the bead I found in my garden. "Look at these. They're from Morocco."

"I'm sure they are."

"They could be!"

We laughed. Laughing with other people, laughing with a companion, made music. He put the beads around my neck. They hung between my breasts and rested on my belly. "They are beautiful. How much for the one of a kind beads from Morocco?"

"A gift for you. Say you'll accept."

"I can't, Clarence."

"But they make you radiant."

"Me? Hardly."

"Take them. I know they make you happy."

They did. "Thank you." I smiled the smile I've always wanted to give to Harold.

Clarence disappeared back into the woods, touching my cheek on purpose as he turned the cart around. He whistled and the old yellow Lab ran up to him and jumped in his bed on the back of the cart. "Good day, ma'am." He touched the brim of his hat like they did in the old movies, and was gone.

Back on my porch alone, I picked up the newspaper again and began to wave it through the air. The beads clicked against each other, the ticking of a clock against my abdomen.

Harold came back from the field earlier than usual that

day.

"Saw you carrying on with that junk man today," he mumbled on his way to the fridge for a beer. He pointed at my beads. "He give you those?"

"No. I bought them."

"Well, I hope you didn't spend too much of my money on some useless ugly beads."

"No, Harold." I sat down and gathered the beads up in my hands. "I didn't spend very much at all."

I can't even break up the last ten years in any recognizable way for you. Used to be that I could say, "Oh yes, that was in '78. Easter time, I think." But not anymore. Even the seasons weren't very real. I knew when they came and I knew when they left. I only marked them by a change of socks. In winter I wore gray socks; in summer I wore blue socks. That was enough definition for me.

Harold marked the seasons too, and after all these years he doesn't much notice them anymore either. He's gotten old, although he doesn't like to admit it. Still says he can knock me down a few pegs if I don't shut up. I know it's not true, but I let him keep thinking it. It seems to give him strength. My strength comes from the quiet. My strength comes from looking out at him over the breakfast table and seeing the shadow of death tapping on his shoulder. My strength comes from anger. He thinks his life's been good. He thinks our life has been good. Tell me what I have to gain by arguing about it now? He's too old to hang out in the bars downtown anymore, and he's too weak to do much about his wandering ways. So now he stays home with me, only now I don't want him to. He just grunts, shifts his pipe in his mouth, and opens another section of the paper. He doesn't notice I'm not talking to him. Actually, I haven't spoken to him in close to three years. He doesn't notice. Which helps me in a way not to notice. Helps me to survive.

I never saw Clarence again. Sometimes I thought of him instead of the stranger at the Greyhound station. Broke up the days. And besides, Clarence had been real. I still wore the beads, even though I'd had to restring them three times since he gave them to me. I guess they don't make things so well in Morocco.

Women outlive men two to one. It's our final moment of peace. I was on the front porch with my coffee when Harold died. Didn't feel a thing. I was daydreaming out across the pine trees, and when I finally got my old butt out of the rocker to go inside, I wondered where Harold was. I hadn't heard him grumbling much lately. I found him, face down at the kitchen table, smoldering pipe on the floor. I didn't have to touch him. I knew. I didn't want to touch him, but I did. I picked up his hand, still slightly warm, barely stiff. No love in those hands. I looked at the lines, the wrinkles, the callouses. Nothing. Empty. Hard. I sat him upright and called the coroner.

After they took his body out of the house and I cleaned up the dishes, I didn't know what I should do. The coroner had touched me on the shoulder and told me he was sorry. Sorry for what, I wondered, but I said thank you, because that's what a person does. Mostly I was thankful the body was out of my kitchen.

I went to the bedroom and pulled out my secret shoe box. The quartz rested on top of a lace doily my grandmother had crocheted. I took it out and rubbed the years away on my apron. I held it up to the sunlight and it glistened so bright it stung my eyes. On the way back to the kitchen, I blinked the dark spots of light away. I lifted the shade and opened the window above the sink. The air tumbled in off the creek, causing my skin to prickle. I placed the quartz on the shelf next to my scarred wooden bead and walked out into the woods. I thought I might find a sprig of mint I could plant in a tiny pot on my sunny windowsill in my very own house.

Vows

$\mathcal{P}$aula wiped her hands on her flowered apron, tossed the dishrag over the faucet, and leaned back on the kitchen counter, surveying her work. Dishes clean. Floor clean. Window clean. Table clean. Everything in its place. The flower arrangement in the center of the table was bright, but not too bright, the largeness of the white iris in the center softened it. She smiled, pleased. Paula had invited her late husband to dinner. She decided it was finally time for some talking. If not forgiveness, then at least some talking. She often wished she could say she killed her husband, but she didn't. He killed himself, some say indirectly, but Paula knew better. He died as a result of his own choices. Just like we all do, when it comes right down to it. He'd been hanging out at a Vietnamese restaurant, playing poker in the back room, talking a little too much. Swaggering a little too much. Someone shot him point blank in the chest. She imagined he never really knew what hit him.

Or at least, if he did, he wouldn't have believed that he was actually going to die. The end of his life was something Ricky Bender had never ever considered.

Paula took off her apron and hung it on the hook beside the refrigerator. Ricky always liked a clean kitchen. His mama's kitchen was always spotless, so, naturally, he assumed that every woman's kitchen would be the same. Paula had different ideas. She didn't like the kitchen. Didn't like cooking. Didn't like Ricky's mama. And, when she really considered it honestly, she didn't like Ricky all that much either. He spit when he got excited. He still rolled his cigarette packages in his shirt sleeves like it was 1956. He shaved every other day and acted like that was a great favor to her. After he died, it took weeks of hot washings to get the cigarette smell out of the bedsheets. Even last night, when she rolled over in the middle of her dreams searching for the warm body that had vanished, she caught a whiff of Pall Mall's that jerked her out of her sleep long enough to believe she heard the water running in the bathroom.

She leaned against the refrigerator. Harvest Gold. A color she has lived long enough to see return to favor. The refrigerator was bare except for two pictures in clear plastic frames — one of Paula and Ricky on a log flume ride at Six Flags Over Georgia, and one of Paula's mother, Rebecca, a daguerreotype faded to yellow, of a young Rebecca holding a single lily, a strand of faux pearls around her neck, looking towards the future with porcelain skin and empty eyes. One day at work, someone had asked Paula if she had any heroes. Paula had thought about it and smiled. "My mother."

Rebecca was many things, but a typical mother was not one of them. She had married a coal miner in Pennsylvania, which left her alone most of the time until the mining accident which left her alone all of the time. Rebecca organized quilting circles, painted the inside of their company-owned house wild shades of indigo and azure. Her house had no curtains. "Let the world see in!" she'd say, spinning through the living room with a dust mop. When Paula was a girl, she was embarrassed by her mother. She wanted someone who worked at the Red Cross, volunteered for the war effort, used linen napkins and made tuna casseroles with crushed Wise potato chips. Instead, her mother made a lot of cheese sandwiches, smoked a lot of cigarettes, wrote reams of poetry and danced with the broom through the house with no curtains to waltzes playing only in her head.

Paula remembered the day the company man came by to tell them there'd been an accident at the mine. It was summer, July, and the air hung thick with mosquitoes. Rebecca had been whistling in the kitchen, chopping lettuce. Paula answered the door. The man was too tall, and he was too wide for his suit. His brown hat was in his hands, and he looked away when Paula opened the door.

"Mama! Mama!" she shouted, slamming the door in the man's face.

Rebecca set the knife down on the counter, wiped her hands on her blue apron, and walked to the door. Paula watched her mother twist her hands like dishrags while the man spoke. She watched while her mother steadied herself against the doorframe. She listened while her mother spoke in low tones to the man, her voice seeming to come from another corner of the room, not from the solid skeleton wearing the blue apron. Rebecca closed the door gently, walked past Paula, and went back to the kitchen. She picked up her knife and began chopping the lettuce in precise movements. Chop! Chop! Scrape. Chop! Chop! Scrape. When Rebecca finally spotted Paula, hiding under the kitchen table staring at her mother's calves, she crouched low to her and said, "Sweetheart, we're on our own now. Your father is dead." Then she rose and washed her hands at the sink.

Paula was paralyzed, her tiny hands wrapped around the metal table legs. Her heart beat too quickly, and she forgot to breathe and became dizzy. She had given her father his lunch pail that morning to take to work. He had grinned and thumped her on the head with his thumb. "Good day, sport," he said, just like he said every morning to her on his way out the door. She always took it to mean he wanted a boy. But now, she clutched the table leg and whispered, "Good day, sport." Her lips formed a pout with the word "sport" and she allowed her lower lip a few seconds of quivering before she swallowed her grief into the tiny room in the middle of her stomach where she pushed everything that did not make her smile.

Chop! Chop! Scrape! Her mother went about making the salad like everything was the same. Paula breathed in deeply, tightened her grip around the table leg and tried to conjure up her father, black miner's hat with the white light on it, dark moustache, hands blackened forever from coal. She remembered pieces, but she couldn't find the whole, and she knew, under the safety of the table, that he had truly disappeared.

Now she knew how it felt to be a widow. She knew how long it took to change habits for two into habits for one. She knew the weight of silence.

Paula straightened the two pictures on her refrigerator. Her mother had been dead for ten years now. She had been living alone. No one found her for three days. Paula went to the burial alone. She tossed her shovel-full of dirt over the casket and drove to Burger King and drank three chocolate milk shakes all in a row. She looked at the two pictures. She was the only one alive in them anymore.

Her house was so quiet her breathing echoed. "OK," she whispered. "Come on, Ricky, it's time." Her gaze roamed the kitchen. No sign of Ricky. He promised he'd come back "to haunt her," he'd say, and laugh. Oh, she thought, he wasn't that bad. He just wasn't for me. That's all. Just wasn't for me.

She decided to make a cup of tea while she waited. Maybe the whistle of the tea kettle would bring him back. "Why do you even want to talk to that man again?" she mumbled. "You've spent half your life trying to get him to pay attention to you, and the other half of your life trying to get rid of him." She pursed her lips. It was true. She didn't even know what really came over her today. Why today was the day. She filled the flower patterned kettle with tap water and placed it on the burner. She reached into the basket beside the stove and selected a Ginseng-Peppermint tea bag.

Perhaps it was last night's dream that convinced her. She'd been travelling through a dark sky bumping into points of stars that ripped her flesh but caused no pain. She travelled straight toward them and as a star tore off her arms, she grew new ones. Over and over all night this happened. When she woke up, her shoulders ached. She thought of her mother again. Funny, how her mother could be dead for ten years and Paula still felt her presence, sometimes stronger now than in life, but Ricky hadn't even been gone six months and it was as if he'd never lived at all. Death isn't better or worse, she thought. It just is. Perception makes the difference.

The kettle whistled and her arm muscles tightened. "It's OK, it's OK," she whispered. "Geez," She poured the hot water into her favorite yellow and black mug and watched the water begin to turn brown from the tea. Ricky hated this mug. Said it reminded him of "bumblebees on acid." She held the warm cup in her palms. There's the nick in the glass where he'd knocked it off the kitchen table one morning. She smirked. He couldn't break it.

Paula sat down at the table to wait. The ticking from the kitchen clock echoed in the stillness. The day they married was one of her happiest memories. She thought she loved him. She did love his dark eyes, long black hair, wide shoulders. She did love the way he gripped her body close under covers of silk and told her she was his fantasy. She loved the way he laughed when he played with the neighbor's German Shepherd and the way he worked weekend after weekend in the garden until the tulips and daisies and daffodils grew in orchestrated abandon, petals a wide open mosaic for the sky. She loved the way he made coffee, perfect every morning, and the way he spent hours trying to fix the grandfather clock that was her family's heirloom. He wouldn't give up until the chimes rang, every thirty minutes, reminding her where she came from.

Hmmmm. She blew on the tea to cool it. She brought the cup to her lips and drank. Ricky Bender. Where the hell are you now? She swallowed. "I've looked for you," she said to the napkin holder. "I've looked for you in the garden, in the garage among the rows of tools and paint. I've looked for you in bed and in my dreams and in my heart, but I can't find you anywhere."

The sun sank, casting wide dark shadows across the room. Paula's hands lay in darkness.

"Daughter,"

"Mama!" Paula dropped the cup on the table. "Mama, where are you?"

"You cannot find in your heart in death what was not in your heart in life."

Paula's heart pounded in her temples. She clenched her jaw. "I loved Ricky. Mama, I did!" The central heating kicked on. "I loved him. I tried. Ricky! Oh God — I should have left you after a year. Why can't I remember you? Why won't you come back? It wasn't all bad, was it?"

The grandfather clock chimed and tears rose behind her eyes. Another hour gone. Wasted. She stood and poured the tea into the sink. The drain gurgled. "You never really loved me either, did you?"

The truth spread through her veins, thick mud, stopping at her heart. Her ears rang. The air felt heavy, a blanket across her shoulders, and she remembered holding on to the metal table leg, so many years ago, and burying her daddy in her body. She held the edge of the counter and shivered as darkness washed across the room. She turned around and on the table lay a single daffodil, its yellow petals already turning brown and brittle along the edges. She picked it up and the petals fell to the floor, one by one, and disappeared into the patterns of the freshly mopped linoleum.

Between Thunder and Lightning

$\mathcal{I}$ laid eyes on you again last summer. The sun was hot, washing over the cotton fields like rain. The air hung like velvet drapes, no breeze, and I sat on my porch fanning myself with an old green church bulletin with one hand, holding a glass of sweet tea in a clear cup with oranges printed on it in the other, when there I saw you, plain as day, sitting in the garden between my rows of tomatoes and cucumbers.

First, I didn't like to believe what I saw. Didn't know what to make of you. You all curled into yourself like a turtle. Your hair was so long I thought it could have been your jacket, but when you shook your head up and your hair fanned down across your shoulders and down your back, I saw that you weren't wearing anything but skin. You crouched low, chest pressed against your knees, bits of green tomato leaves glowing against your skin.

"Shirley!" I shouted.

172

Jack heard me from inside the house. "Who you talkin' to out there?"

"No one," I said. "Just myself."

But you were still there, looking at me with all the fire and spark you had when you were living. I'd know you anyplace, daughter. Anyplace.

"Shirley." This time I whispered. "Come on over here and talk to your mama."

But you didn't move, except maybe to stretch out your leg, or to shield your eyes from the dripping sun. You arched your back against the tomato stakes, and I saw how beautiful your body was — young, tanned brown as Sunday biscuits, skin shimmering with sweat.

"Mama love me." That's what you said to me. I can still hear it in my heart. "Mama love me." You said it just like that too. Like a fact. Like something important I'm supposed to instantly know.

"Mama does love you, sweet pea."

"Mama love me." And you wrapped your hair around your face and hid your blue blue eyes from me. The red earth beneath your feet crumbled into hard chunks that became dust that floated up around you like a shroud.

I remembered the day in June a few years back when you jumped into a creekbed that was too shallow and landed smack on your backside in that same red clay. Like to have tattooed that color on your flesh! Mmmm. Made me smile just to remember. Lord, made me smile.

I heard the pipes squeak. Jack must've turned on the water in the house. That man was always running the water. He'd take perfectly clean dishes out of the cupboards just to have something to wash. Especially since you gone and left us, Shirley-girl. That man don't know what to do with himself, so

Laraine Herring 173

he does dishes. Drove me crazy, but soon enough I just learned to appreciate that someone else besides me was doing the dishes. I wanted to go inside and fetch him — tell him he had to come outside and see his dead daughter sitting naked in the garden, but I wasn't sure exactly how a person goes about starting a conversation like that.

Thunder danced behind me. You looked up, waiting for the lightning. You never believed me when I told you that the lightning came first. When you were living, I'd sit next to you on your bed when it got cloudy and you could smell that first hint of damp coming from the west.

"See, Shirley, storm's coming. You can tell how far away it is by counting between the lightning and the thunder." You were about eight that night we sat up and watched the storm, you all snug and comfy under your great-grandma's quilt. "One, two, three...here that thunder now? That means the storm's three miles away."

"Is that far?" you asked.

"Yes, that's far." I said and stroked your silky hair. But three miles was barely a blip. You went where I couldn't find you. Not ever. Not until now.

The pine trees rustled me out of my memory. You cupped your hands over your ears so the thunder wouldn't scare you. You always told me you could feel it rumble in the pit of your stomach. "Like when I eat too much chili, mama." That's what you said to me. Like too much chili.

So hot, there on my porch that afternoon. My blue cotton dress stuck to my legs and arms and sometimes you looked blurry to me with all the sweat pouring into my eyes. Come to think of it, you looked blurry in life to me sometimes too — always moving so fast, running from here to there, tracking your young muddy feet on my white carpet. Mmm. I like to think of you moving so fast. Tell me, how fast can you move now?

You stood up in my tomato patch. How is it you're here? I reached for you. I wanted to hold you in my arms again, smell the musky scent of your skin, run my fingers over your tangled hair. The wind pushed me back into my chair. Clouds covered the sun. I saw you, standing straight, hair whipping across your face, covering it until I could only see the tip of your nose.

Oh, Shirley, honey, you don't know how much I miss you. Walking around this house now, without you, I just wander most of the time. Make sure Jack's fed and the cat's fed and I'm fed. That's about all, darlin'. Now that we don't hear your giggling from the top of the stairs on Saturday morning. Now that we don't give evil eyes to the little boys who picked you daisies with the roots still hanging from the stems. Now that we don't have anyone to really look at but each other.

Your daddy misses you too, sweet pea, but he won't never say it. It's just not his way. You got to respect that about a person. Your daddy and I are too young, child, to be broken like this.

Lightning cut through the dark sky, and you froze, a startled kitten. I saw your lips forming the words, "One, two, three, four..." and then the rumble came, and you held your hands tight against your belly and closed your eyes.

The night you died was stormy like this. Worse, actually. We were getting the tail end of a hurricane. When I looked out your bedroom window I saw trees bending every which way, but when I listened, everything was strangely silent. All I heard was the pounding of the rain, the growling of the thunder, and the raspy gasp of your breath. I held your hand as you lay in your bed, your body shivering with fever and cough that the doctor swore to me would break by dawn.

"Pneumonia doesn't get us anymore," the doctor told me,

handing me a bottle of penicillin, and I lapped up the rhythm of those words.

I held your sweaty hand tight as I dared, and when the lightning broke the dimness of your room, I saw you whisper, "One, two..." and before you could say three, your breath rattled out of your dry lips and you left me.

Your daddy and I buried your ashes in the backyard, next to Murphy, your very first puppy. I planted a cherry tree over top of you both, and I water it every day. Won't that make you happy, Shirley, darling? To be resting under shade and pretty blossoms?

I shook my head and rubbed my eyes, still unwilling to believe I saw you in front of me. My tears mixed with the first droplets of rain and I felt the steam of my breath hot against my open lips.

"The storm is close, Mama," you said, gripping the tomato stake.

"Yes, baby," I ran toward the garden now, not caring that the wind had picked up once again. Not caring that the rain pelted my body with hard cold drops.

I fell on my knees, crushing some of my cucumbers. I opened my arms and this time you fell willingly into them. You covered my quivering body with your hair, and your tiny naked arms squeezed my neck tight. You smelled of patchouli oil. "Love *you* Mama."

"I love you, baby. So much." I held you closer, wanting to absorb you into my flesh. Wanting to give you the air from my very own lungs.

Lightning illuminated the yard, and I thought of the too bright too white searchlights those car dealers on Hawthorne Street always use.

You clutched my hair and whispered, "One, two..." and

left me, again, sitting in the dark, as the thunder broke me open at my ribs, and the rain poured in and washed me clean away.

Cinnamon and Honeysuckle

Lordy be, I think I see old Jebediah Prange now. Comin' up the drive. That man — always a sinister look about that Negro hoodoo man— with his scarred face from the time a chicken foot he was usin' in some spell or somethin' wasn't quite ready to participate on ol' Jeb's terms. Them chicken feet commenced to carryin' on all over his body. Tore him up right good. Good 'nough to where folks thought he might not make it, and them souls that believe in the hoodoo made quite a commotion around his shack till five days later he walked out good as new. 'Cept for the scars on his face. They never heal. That little show done more for his reputation than his entire lifetime of tricks. Now, though, if'n I didn't know, and exceptin' for the scars on his face of course, ol' Jeb looks quite normal, walkin' down my driveway, ol' raggedy hat in his hands. Yep. Looks like he could be a regular person. I don't care. I don't trust no hoodoo. Gives me the willies. Ever since I was a young 'un. Don't mean I don't believe. No sir, I believes. That's exactly why I gets the willies.

"Afternoon, Coolidge," Jebediah walks himself right up on my porch and sets himself down. "Mind if I set a spell?" 'Course, he asks this after he done set himself down. He knows I notice.

"Of course not, Jebediah. Makes yourself at home. Can I offer ya some whiskey?" I hand him the bottle I been suckin' on most of the day.

"No, thank you. I comes on business."

"Business?" I take a swig. The whiskey is warm and wet and goes down like a $20 whore at midnight. "I hope you didn't come to put no spell on me. I minds my own business."

Jebediah kinda laughs from somewhere deep in his chest. Somewhere spooky. "Now Coolidge, don't you worry about that. If I put the magic on you, you won't even know I been here." He swings one giant leg up over the other one and gets comfy. "I come on behalf of Heddy."

"Heddy?" I take me another swallow. For once, the second time ain't smoother. Heddy Johnson. One fine lady she was. She rather took a fancy to me. I never could figure out why, but she was hog bound and determined she was going to get a ring on my finger. Quite obviously, she didn't, but Lordy could she cook up a fine mess of collards and she was not opposed to *any* of the pleasures of the flesh, if you catch my meaning. Ah Heddy. I spent myself many a magic evening with that woman. Finally she gave up on me and quit coming around. See, she gave me an ultimatum, but I never have responded well to any sorta demand from a woman, so I told her if that's what she was after, she could just get on down the road. I was more than a little surprised that she did. Heard tell she died a month or so ago. Fluid in her chest.

She never did marry. I like to think she never could find

another fella to replace me, but the older I gets, the more I learn and I figure she finally realized she really didn't have no real use for us menfolk. Seems like if I ran the world, I'd have men and women living on separate sides of the street, getting together on special days to fulfill our mutual needs and then getting back on with the business of living. I do wish I'd've known she was dying. I'd have gone to be by her. A lady as fine as that one was ought not to die alone. Though I reckon when you get right down to the heart of things, we all die alone. Should've been there to hold her hand. I could have kept her from being afraid. Woman like Heddy — I know she's got a clear path to the Heavenly Father because she didn't ever know any true joy on earth and that's what the Scriptures tell us. "Blessed are the sorrowful." Or something like that. Me on the other hand, I'm not so clear on the matters of my eternal soul. Reckon we aren't supposed to know the answers to them things.

"I reckon you know Miss Heddy passed on." Jebediah says.

"I know. God rest her soul." I think back to the day Heddy died to kinda imagine what it must've been like for her, and I reckon she'd gotten up 'fore sunup like everyday to make the coffee in that old tarnished silver pot that belonged to her Mammy. She probably made too much, like she always done, so in case somebody came callin' she'd have a nice hot beverage to serve them. "Jebediah, if I'd have known sooner I'd've gone to be by her."

"There weren't no need for you to be by her. I was there."

"Mmmm." I stiffen up inside, like I really am nothin' but bones.

"She always spoke kindly of you."

"I'd heard tell she'd taken up with you, but for the life of me, I couldn't figure it out."

"I thought you'd known by now." Jeb's voice is so soft at first I think he didn't speak at all.

"Thought I'd know what?" This is getting tiresome. The sun's beating down so hard on my tin roof I halfs expect the roof to melt and trickle smooth and silver down the post like rain. I wipe my forehead with the back of my hand and flick the sweat from my fingers onto the red ground.

"She made compromises, Coolidge. She was a good woman. Only I was the compromise. You were the first choice."

I'm feelin' so guilty I think my stomach's goin' to explode all over Jebediah and his fancy sentences. "Heddy known what kinda man I was when she took up with me. She know'd I weren't goin' to settle down. She know'd I's always going to choose my banjo over her. I didn't lead that woman on, Jebediah Prange, and I'll thank you not to go makin' anymore accusations on my own porch."

"I didn't make any accusations. I said a fact. You were Heddy's first choice. Always were. Nothin' I could do about it. I comes to find out why, Coolidge, why you could let her go and let her go to come to me?"

"I don't know as I let her go. She left me, if you recall."

"I recall that she had no options. A woman's got to have options."

"She gave me an ultimatum, man! She told me to marry her. She told me!" I swallow what feels like half the bottle of whiskey. "You know that don't fly."

Jeb nods. At least I think he does. He doesn't seem real, sittin' there all cool and collected, his hat still in his hand, watchin' me get all worked up.

"I don't see why you're here talkin' to me about all this now. Heddy done been dead over a month. Why didn't you come a-callin' when she was livin'?"

"Why didn't you?" He looks at me and kinda squeezes his left eye a little so he can look like he's really tryin' to listen to me.

"Go on, man. Get off my property. I got me some things to do."

Jeb just sits there. Aggravatin' and silent.

"Fine. Sits there all you want. I'm goin' inside."

"I come to give you this." Jeb reaches deep into his overall pockets and pulls out a fat crumpled envelope. From where I'm sittin', the envelope looks yellow.

"What's that?" I ain't goin' any closer to him than I have to.

"It's from Heddy. She asked that I take it to you once she gone."

Now I'm mad. "She been dead a month! Where you been?"

"I didn't want to see you right off." Jeb reaches for my whiskey and drinks long and hard. His body don't even flinch as it's goin' down. I set up and take notice. "You may not want to hear me out, Coolidge, but I loved that woman. Whether I was her second choice or not. By God, I loved her."

We sit in silence for what must be my whole lifetime, but I reckon it's just been a few minutes. I feel two drops of sweat trickle down my neck and meet at the small of my back. You know that place where can't no one reach but your mama and your woman. Heddy used to rub store-bought lotion into my back and she would start right at that place. I used to get all over her. Tellin' her a man's got enough trouble in this world without smellin' like a damn flower patch, but I secretly loved it. I loved her thick calloused hands pressing hard against probably the only part of my body that was still smooth. Still open.

Neither Jeb nor me says much. It's as if we're suddenly

aware of who we are. Two old men who loved the same woman. The same dead woman. Jeb lets the envelope fall from his hand and I reach to pick it up, much like I had only dropped a pencil, or maybe I was just stretching my arms like I did Lord some thirty years ago when I was hopin' to pull a sweet sweaty young thing closer to me. Jeb is at least polite enough to act like he don't notice me. Me and my "patterns" as Heddy always say. "You got the darndest patterns," she'd mouth off after I made a big production out of leavin' my boots outside the front door with the toes facing each other. My granddaddy taught me that for good luck and to keep the spirits away. Or if I hangs all my clothes in the closet accordin' to color. "Patterns. You sure got you some strange patterns, Coolie. Yes, you do." Long about this time, I'd grab her around her rolling waist and pull her close to me and breathe in her smell. She was one of them women who didn't have a real distinctive smell. Sometimes it was like cinnamon. Sometimes honeysuckle. But I sure did know when it wasn't there. Lord knows I did know when it wasn't there.

The envelope was indeed yellow, but it was yellow like from cookin' grease or rust on the bottom of an old Ford pick-up that's been settin' up in somebody's front yard a mite too long. There was my name. Coolie. I'd've known her handwriting anywhere — even after all this time from seein' her grocery lists or the little notes she'd make on the tissue paper thin edges of her King James family Bible. I didn't understand why she always made them little notes to herself. I thought the book was supposed to tell you everything you needed to know. But now I'm startin' to think there's lots of stuff I just didn't know all that much about. Coolie — my name — is underlined twice. Wonder if that means somethin'. Funny how the most simple things become so complicated once the body doin' the thing is dead.

Laraine Herring

"Aren't you goin' to open it?" Jeb's voice is creaky now, like when you just wake up in the mornin' and don't really want to be speakin' to nobody.

"I'm a-fixin' to. It's addressed to me." If I'd've been in Jebediah's position, I'd've done opened this letter and sealed it back up. I think that must be one of the more meaningful revelations about myself. Jeb doesn't answer me. I turn the envelope over. I can see the streaks of dirt from her fingers along the seal. There's almost one complete fingerprint. I reckon it must be her right forefinger. I run the envelope under my nose — see if I can catch a whiff of her, but I can't. Whatever it was she smelled like traveled only on her flesh. Didn't want nothin' to do with paper. There's somethin' hard and round in the envelope. I try to figure out what it might be. Try to put off openin' the letter as long as I can. Don't rightly know why. Though I get the feelin' Jebediah knows why.

"Yours was the last name she spoke." Jeb's not lookin' at me, so I ain't entirely sure I heard right.

"What?"

"'Coolidge.' That's what she said. You were her last word."

I stare at Jeb, who just looks right past me up over to the Fulton farm, which is almost a mile from here and all's you can really see is the smoke from their chimney, so I figure he's deliberately trying to ignore me. His eyes are black now, and suddenly icy. I can almost see ice crystals formin' on his eyelashes. I think for one monumental moment how he must feel. Hoodoo man or no hoodoo man, nobody wants to be runner up. I sort of feel sorry for him, sittin' there all cold and stiff, bringing me the letter from the woman he loved. No kinda spell in the world can make a man get over the love of a good woman. I didn't really know that until right now. Didn't even really know how much I loved her till right now. Till old Jebediah come walkin'

184   *Monsoons*

down my driveway draggin' her ghost behind him.

"Reckon a man's got a right to some privacy on his own porch."

Jeb don't make a move. "I ain't lookin' over your shoulder. I reckon I got a right too — seein' as I'm the one who carried it to you."

I can't argue with him. Hell, I agree with him. And I'd have almost changed positions with him he sounded so lonely right then. Almost. I slide my finger under the flap, delicate like, like I's pettin' a kitten right down its spine. The paper inside has raggedy edges, the kind from spiral notebooks from the drugstore. The blue lines on it have smeared so much the paper almost looks blue. I wonder just how long Mr. Hoodoo Man's been carryin' it around in his pocket. I look up at Jeb, whose mind's still off somewhere over the Fulton's corn crop. I wonder if he can remember what it is Heddy smelled like. A gold wedding band falls into my hand. I'm so surprised I almost drop it through the porch cracks. I fold open the letter.

Coolie,

I thought one day I'd put this on your finger, but that ain't so. This ring was my papa's. I took it when he died to give to the man I love. That's you. Case you didn't know.

Love Always,

Heddy Johnson

Jeb clears his throat somethin' fierce. Mr. Hoodoo Man, I think, you so good you already knows what this says. But for once I'm smart enough to just think it. I offer him some more of my whiskey, but he ignores me. He wants me to tell him what's in the letter. I think of Heddy writing it. She loved writing and practiced makin' letters all over the place. Whenever she had the chance. She thought writing somethin' down made it so. Made it factual.

Somethin' hot and thick is pullin' up in my throat. I cough real quick and stand up. Jeb doesn't make a move. I remember Heddy's smile. She smiled a lot. She had this big gap between her front teeth. Lots of women would've been embarrassed by that. Not Heddy. She'd smile just as beautiful as a queen. More beautiful 'cause she's smilin' at me. I see her smilin' at me now, handin' me a plate full of pancakes or givin' me that naughty look she had when she needed some lovin'. I'm sure sorry Heddy. I did know you loved me. I only didn't know I loved you.

Lordy be, if Jeb don't want none of my whiskey, I sure do. I swallow what's left. "I'm glad you were there for her, Jebediah." He still don't move. "Hey, I'm sorry for your loss, man."

Jeb stands up. "Naw, Coolidge. I'm sorry for *your* loss." He pushes his hat down on his head and wanders off down the driveway. He don't look back at me, settin' on the porch with Heddy's ghost. That's what he done. He done brought her ghost to my house. I try to put the ring on my finger. It don't fit and gets stuck at my knuckle. I pull it back off and slide it back in the yellow envelope. Damn, Heddy! I told you who I was! I always told you who I was!

The wind picks up, blowin' pine needles and the smells from the Fulton place across my property. I catch a whiff of cinnamon and set up. Heddy? That you? Heddy? As quick as it come, the wind die down. I shove her letter deep in the pocket of my work pants and settle back down in my chair. If I kick back far enough, I can still see Jebediah's back as he walks on down the road, wind playin' with his hat all friendly like. I reckon he can smell the cinnamon too. And if I knows old Jebediah Prange, he's laughin' at me, from someplace dark at the center of his soul.

Signatures

for dad

The sun is yellow as ripe banana
and I am the tallest person on the beach
sitting squarely on the center of your shoulders.

I pedal wildly fast safe on training wheels
I did not know you had removed before
you pushed me forward.

You called me writer and pasted my first story
penciled on large brown paper on the fridge
and read it out loud to me so I could hear my words.

We sat in the car once before the end
and talked of love. You said you knew nothing of it
except that it is all that is.

Time does not heal all wounds. Time allows
the water to flow over the jagged edges long enough
to smooth the edges into thick, blue-black scars.

Once, I caught you in the kitchen after midnight
eating Sara Lee chocolate cake
letting the cat lick the icing from your fork.

You listened to Kingston Trio albums after dinner and said you
played them on the jukebox at UNC before you knew anything
about anything, when tomorrow was still a collage of color.

You took me driving in the mountains north of our house.
We flew over wild turns and hills. I didn't know where we were.
But you did.

We sat in the car listening to Elvis on the radio. "I've never heard this one," you said. "I thought I knew all of his songs."
You turned up the volume and cried.

Sometimes now I still see you sitting on the couch
with an iced tea. But when I reach for your hand, all I feel is warm wet air and the aching space in between my ribs.

The wind blows furious around me
and I stand strong and silent in the center
aware, ever aware, of the absence of you.

How do you know when you're looking at someone
for the last time? You feel it. They touch your hand
and linger, flesh on flesh, just a little too long.

The Veil

$\mathcal{I}$n the playground of my childhood elementary school, the air smells of wet woolen socks stuffed into laundry hampers. The trees hang brittle branches draped with moss across the narrow footpath. Years before, before Reaganomics, before computer ping pong, before Elvis died, the path was four feet wide, rimmed every quarter mile with wooden markers etched with big numbers. Tiny metal signs poked out of the red North Carolina soil identifying poison ivy, or oak trees, or telling us to look out for king snakes.

Now, a crushed Miller Lite can rests off to the side, cocooned in a thick spider's web. A giant tree, struck by lightning, blocks the path in front of me. Lichen covers its bark and ants pour across its surface like water. The woods buzz. I look around me for the mosquitoes I know are here, but I couldn't see them. Not until I ride back to the hotel, counting the bites, would I have proof that they had even been there at all.

These woods border my elementary school. Although only half a block deep, they were a source of endless mystery to me as a child. My best friend and I would cut through the woods on the way home each day, believing it saved precious moments. We sought sanctuary among the trees when the school kids had acted like school kids. On Saturdays, I would take my notebook and my all-time favorite book, *Harriet the Spy*, and read and make notes under the shade of the tallest oak. I would crush black ants and red ants, and the eternal enigma, the red and black ants who tried to take my space. I never won, and after an hour or so had to give up and move to a bench.

I saw my first Hustler magazine in those woods. Pages had been torn and crumpled and left in the tree branches. My friend and I found them and opened them with delicious anticipation. We saw images of naked women, bottoms in the air, with things I had never seen before stuck in them. Women with their mouths open and eyes closed, faces covered in a gooey white film. We threw the pictures down. I swallowed.

"That's nasty," my friend said.

"Yeah," I said. "You don't think that's really what it is, do you?"

We sat in somber silence, weighing the evidence. "It must be," she said. "why else would they print it?"

I was stumped. "I don't know." I tried to imagine someone sticking something into me down there. I couldn't even try. "Mom says it feels good."

"You asked her?"

I nodded. "I wanted to know."

My friend's green eyes widened. "Wow. I don't think my mom and dad do it at all."

I thought about it. "Probably not," I reasoned. After all, my friend was adopted.

"We should go," she said.

"Yeah."

And we stood up, brushed the dry leaves and pine needles from our clothes, and followed the path to the paved opening in front of our street. We walked in silence, each of us picturing ourselves as the women in the photos. Each of us terrified of growing up.

Back before global warming, the hostage crisis in Iran, the Gulf War and a trillion dollar deficit, I lived in a brick house with red shutters on the top of a hill. We had a row of prickly berry bushes edging the sidewalk, and the driveway was so steep my dad would fall walking to get the paper when the ice was too thick. Mom sewed orange and brown curtains for the kitchen windows, and when I would lay on the damp grass by the sidewalk and make cloud pictures, I could see my mother, upside down, watching from the window above the sink. We had a sliding glass door that led out to a red wooden porch where the Hibachi lived. When I was even younger I would ride my tricycle in circles over the planks. "Ah-thumpety-thump thump thump." Dad would say as I rode. "Thump thump thump. Choo-choo!" I would giggle and ride even faster around and around, believing I was getting somewhere. We had a black cat named Charley who lived in my grandmother's old butter churn. Sometimes, when no one was looking, I let Charley in the house, admiring his ebony fur against the tan tile of the den.

My dad laughed in rich tones, low C's and E's. His skin was ruddy from playing golf in the sun. The muscles in his arms were thick and hard, to compensate for his left leg, which had been eaten by polio. He sat in his brown leather LaZy-boy chair and laughed at Archie Bunker. My sister and I would hide out in the hallway and watch TV over his shoulder until we would fall asleep in our footed pajamas.

Before breast implants and space probes to Mars, my dad helped me write my first story. I wrote about a kitty who was left behind when her family moved. I wrote of the kitty's journey to find her family. I wrote of the kitty's sadness. He joined my sentences together, helped shape the plot, and taught me how to uncover the title.

Now, so many years later, I don't know what I thought I would find in these woods. I had dreamed of them at night, in my home on my pink flannel sheets two thousand miles away from the little brick house on the hill. I had dreamed of the trees, their branches dark with rain, bending and scratching at my window. Begging me to come back.

Today it is overcast and humid. It is Sunday morning. My old elementary school doubles as a Baptist church. People pour out from the blue doors that led to my third grade classroom. They laugh and shake hands in the parking lot where I learned to ride my red bike. They climb into their sport utility vehicles and merge onto the street where I walked with my grandmother one Easter many years ago. I had worn the blue polka-dotted dress she made for me and I got us lost in the neighborhood. When we finally found the brick house on the hill, we were hungry and thirsty and had blisters on our baby toes.

The tree where I read *Harriet the Spy* and chased ants is still here. Blue-green lichen dots the bark. The tree used to be in the center of the playground, but now the monkey bars and swingsets have been moved to government-approved playground surfacing, leaving only the trees in their bed of sand and gravel. I press my back against the thick trunk and slide down between the roots. A sharp pebble burrows into my spine and I shift my weight and lean my head back, looking up through the web of leafy branches at the shifting gray clouds. There's a mountain goat. There's a sunflower. There's a balloon. The wind caresses my face, delicate fingers tickling my skin.

My legs stick straight out in front of me, and when I look at my feet my black boots become my red Keds sneakers with the white tips. My maroon, rayon matched outfit becomes my denim gauchos and orange T-shirt. I hear screaming from the field behind me. Kids playing T-ball. Mothers screaming support for their babies as they run around the bases. Fathers coaching from the lawn chairs. I see behind closed eyes the white and brown station wagons filled with golden retrievers, plastic bats and whiffle balls. I see kites, colored red, white and blue, dancing in the sky. I see my mom and dad watching me lose the long-jump on Field Day and I see my self, forfeiting official membership in the Clean Plate Club because I refuse to eat the baked beans they served with the hot dogs and chocolate milk.

The gravel is uncomfortable, just as I'd remembered. I open my eyes and brush black ants off my shins. The clouds break apart, speckling the sky with patches of blue. The parking lot is empty now. Church over. The field is silent and empty. A bluejay cackles in the branches above me. I stretch my arms above my head and wrap them around the tree. When I remove them, pieces of bark cling to my palms. I pick them off slowly, gently, and stand up. The wind stops. My skin is sticky and my lower back aches.

I look back to the parking lot. My midsized efficiency rental car is still there. I know my matching set of luggage is in the hotel room. I had left my cosmetic bag open on the sink. The magnetic room key rests in my jacket pocket. I have money in my wallet. Money in the bank. A job to go home to. Still, I search the schoolyard for the sand patch I tried to jump over. I listen for the voices of the children in my class. I sniff the air for burgers cooking on the Hibachi on the red porch in the back-yard of the brick house.

I only see a run-down blue school, classrooms branching into clusters of darker blue trailers. I see a playground with stacked tires and graffiti stamped picnic benches. I hear cars speeding down the residential streets, occasional bird songs, the scampering of squirrels. I smell only dampness, wet leaves, old metal. If I had my spiral bound college ruled notebook, I would have written in all caps like Harriet the Spy:
WOODS FAMILIAR. TREES CALLING. GHOSTS EVERYWHERE.

I would then close my spiral bound college ruled notebook, if I had it, sliding the blue Bic ball point pen into the spine, and walk through the woods home for lunch of bologna and cheese, or maybe liverwurst if mom had just come back from Bi-Lo. I would turn south toward the trees, scratch a few ant bites, push my glasses up the bridge of my nose, and walk.

But that would have been 20 years ago. Today, I brush the gravel off my matched rayon outfit. My contacts are comfortable in my eyes. My notebook is in my mind and there are no ant bites. Still, I walk south, towards the woods.

They have thinned. I can see the street on the other side now. I can see the whole arc of the path, starting and ending at the playground. The loop that took us on mysteries and games of hide and go seek is no more than a few hundred yards at best. No more mysterious than shaved ice. The path has not been kept up. Wild grasses grow along the edges, ivy crosses it. Bark and leaves are ground into mulch under my feet. The earth is wet. The two-inch heels on my black boots sink. The air presses against my skin like too many quilts on a warmer than expected winter morning. The clouds cover up the sun, and every few minutes I hear "drip-drip" as water slides off the branches and hits the piles of dead leaves. The trees tick and snap as the wind

Laraine Herring   *195*

or an animal passes through them. I breathe — really breathe in the green leaves, the rotten bark, the fermenting beer, the bird feces. The air is warm, almost hot, and I feel it in my blood-stream.

Thunder rumbles low. I feel it through the soles of my feet.

"Sugar," my father, dead before the end of Reaganomics, calls to me.

Rainwater slips off an oak leaf and lands on the bridge of my nose, right where my glasses would have rested.

"Sugar,"

I spin around. A crumpled piece of loose leaf paper dances across the playground on the wind. A car honks. I press my hand against my pocket and feel the credit card sized room key. I breathe, open mouthed, and close my eyes. My heart pounds. I count to three, open my eyes and watch a mosquito on my forearm. The mosquito bites me before I exhale and blow him away.

"Sugar,"

He is in front of me. Palpable. The trees shimmer. My lips thicken and dry. My tongue is cotton. A thin film of sweat coats my face.

"Dad?" The word chokes me, a rock in my abdomen.

A breeze touches my cheek, fingertips on my eyelids, flesh on flesh. Breath in my ear. Hot blood squeezing my heart. Dad's arms are thick as I remembered, his flesh ruddy from golf-ing in the sun. His eyes blue tourmaline, his pupils black onyx. He blinks slowly. My eyes burn, a hand squeezes my heart. I tilt my head, rolling it slowly side to side, breathing in Mennen, Aquafresh and sweat.

"Sugar,"

I smell hamburgers on the Hibachi. Fresh cut grass and

dried leaf piles. Fred, the horny toad who lived under the sidewalk by the back stairs hops across the concrete. Charley looks up at me with yellow eyes framed by soft black fur and rubs around my ankles. My glasses are heavy on my nose, the lenses steamed in the upper corners. My bookbag hangs limp down my arm, the maroon spelling book sticking out of the top. My red Keds are untied and I watch dad leaning against the chain link fence, talking about adult things, flicking the ashes from his Pall Mall onto the driveway. The robins have built a new nest in the cherry tree by the side door. I could smell the cherry blossoms, touch their silky petals. I remembered I had a test on the capitols of the fifty states. I couldn't remember the capitol of Wyoming.

The wind turns cold and presses icy needles against my neck. The hair on my neck prickles. I shiver and move forward into the heat in front of me. The humidity exhales.

"Sugar," he whispers. I smell peanut butter, fresh tomatoes, fig preserves and A-1 steak sauce.

"Daddy, oh daddy," My body shakes from the soles of my feet. The air quivers. I inhale chunks of thick buzzing oxygen. My lungs ache. I reach out my hand, eyes closed, and for a heartbeat, for the moment between blinking and opening, I touch his cheek, hot, warm and living. I cup my hand and catch nothing but air and thin silk from a spider's web.

I open my eyes. Cloudy sky. Faint thunder. Thick trees. Red moist mud. An earthworm and a moth and nothing in front of me but me.

Whispering Pines

Today old Joleen Jones buried her last living friend, Mr. Barnard. They'd dated some, after Joleen's husband Gordon died. But of course, she'd never crossed the line. She couldn't figure out why she cared so much about being faithful to Gordon now that he was dead. Well, none of the past matters much now. She is the last one.

She sits out on her front porch on the $5 white and green patio chair she bought at the Zayre store before it went out of business. Her knee-highs are rolled down to her ankles, which today are more swollen than usual. It is one of those perfectly still days. The kind when you're not even sure your breath is moving. Joleen thinks she can see the marsh grass bending a bit across the pier, but she can't be sure. Her vision is not what it used to be.

She smooths her pale blue housedress across her knees and stares at the acres of pine trees surrounding her house.

Gordon built this house, high up on cement blocks so that when the creek rose, the house stayed dry. Joleen had lived on this land for sixty-three years. Still doesn't quite feel like hers.

If she closes her eyes and frees herself a little bit, she can hear the sounds of her life in the cries of the osprey and the swamp frogs. She can hear the voices of her son, Gordon Junior, and her husband playing in the pines. Hunting quail or playing hide and seek. Today is her favorite kind of day. Overcast. The kind of day where no one expects much out of you. You can kind of sit on your porch, alone, and think and listen.

The wind picks up and she turns her craggy face towards it. She used to tell Junior that the wind came from an ancient blue man who lived in the clouds. That was pretty much the extent of her imagination, but she had tried.

Maybe now Junior knows where the wind comes from. It's been nine years since he died. Six since Gordon. Sometimes she can't remember what they sound like. She thinks she hears them sometimes, calling to her in the night, but when she wakes up and calls back to them, all she hears is silence.

Something crashes inside the house. Startled, she turns away from the wind and walks inside. There, sitting at her dining room table are Gordon and Junior. Shimmering like asphalt in the summer, they rock back on the dining room chairs and stare at her. She drops her glass of iced tea on the carpet.

"Mother," says her son. "Come. Play checkers with us."

"Jesus Christ," she says. A prayer. She doesn't take her Lord's name in vain.

"Come sit down, Joleen," says Gordon. "You can be red."

She sits, stares, reaches toward them, but they shake their heads. "You can't touch."

She can see the color of their eyes. Father, son, eyes blue as the wind man in the clouds. "Why are you here?" The wind

Laraine Herring   *199*

picks up outside. She hears the tree branches scraping the sides of the house.

"I'll go first," says Junior.

Joleen sits, shifts her weight in the high-backed mahogany chair and looks at her two visitors. The ghost of her son reaches out his bony fingers and slides a black checker over one space to the left. He meets his mother's eyes and speaks from beneath the earth. "Your move." The ghost of her husband rests his skeletal hand on his son's shoulder.

Outside the clapboard house, the wind weaves through the pine branches. Whispering pines, they used to call them. She thinks she remembers a song — a whining banjo-picking bluesy number from a time when every race had a perceived place. From a time when crawdads were still on the menu at Mildred's and coffee was a beverage not a pastime. Johnny Horton? She can't be sure.

She can't be sure of very many things these days. She looks through the ghost of her son to the newly upholstered Victorian sofa. Its right claw is still chipped from when her son had fallen, back in 1944, playing too fast with his trucks. She did remember that. The scar on his temple never vanished. She can still see it, in fact, on the side of his shimmering skull.

"Your move," Junior speaks again, this time from the attic, from beneath the worn yellow and red copy of *Little Black Sambo*, from under the trunk with his toy trucks and report cards.

She sees the soul of her husband whispering into the heart of her son. They face her. She looks through them, through a fuzzy hazy blurry spectre of who they once were. But she sees them clearly for the first time. Now. Across the checkerboard on an overcast weighty day. Three old souls playing checkers. Two dead men and one live screaming kicking no longer bleeding no longer part of the life circle woman.

The man on the right had pushed himself into her, and she pushed the man on the left out of her, and that was that. That was her life. Now, flesh hangs from her fingers like melting icicles. She reaches toward a red checker, hesitating above it, hovering like the sand fleas in the backyard over the pier. Her husband and her son watch her fingers. Through their hazy essence their memories appear to her, inverted right angles, prismacolors of what should have been.

"Mo - o - o - o - ther!"

The fiery howl from the eye of the hurricane of his soul blows open her life, a blank book, edges gilded in blood, chapters scratched out, erased, missing, heart page jagged.

She trembles. The pages rustle. She looks to her husband for what she did not know, but he couldn't reach her. He reaches for his son and the two become one. As it was in the beginning. She imagines these two beings locked in flesh, young flesh, for that is how they live still inside her. New. Unscarred. By her or anyone.

There is no guidance for this in the Bible. Ashes to ashes. Sweep the dust under an imported Asian tapestry rug, vacuum and move on. Joleen learned that she could bury mistakes under her rug, but then she had to track the dust of her past through every clean whitewashed wall of her future.

This time the past had come back for her. She thinks she'll get up and take the roast out of the oven. Then, she will sit in her rocking chair and watch the sun reflecting off the Inland Waterway. There would be no more ghosts. Only memories. Memories she could control.

She tries to stand, but the ghosts blow her back, their breath fastening around her like a seatbelt, locking her into the game. She pushes a red checker forward — the only direction she could, and hopes she's not devoured by the howling hearts of family.

Muse

I.

Today the ghosts have names.
There's Celia in her treehouse,
Billie, pushing wire-rimmed glasses up his nose,
Kathy, still with bent spine and crutches, and oh,
Delilah.
Of course, there's always Delilah.
She's got huge warm wet lips
And a snaking slithering body
That dances rings around my belly.
She whispers in my ear
when all the world is sleeping.
She tells me,
"Walk." And so I do.
I rise and follow her to her house
where single colors blend into rainbows
into comets into shooting stars
and she is at home
in purple flowing gown
dangling earrings
sexy smile.
She wants to take me out so far
that when I look through my eye sockets
I see the bones of my skull
and I feel instantly the difference
between body and spirit and I know
that this skeleton is just a frame.

A magical organic entity that covers
ancient warrior marks.
Delilah does the two-step and the jitterbug
and she smells of molasses and collards.
Her house is covered with crooked vines and is
guarded by a ten-foot king snake named Larry.
The porch steps are rickety and the screens
have long since fallen into dust.
An old white rocker sits next to a rusty
washboard, connected to the wooden floorboards
by the web of Grandmother Spider.
Inside, the dirt floor is muddy from the river.
The house floods twice a year, spring and fall,
Renewing and releasing.
The faucet drips iron-rich water into the rusted sink while
Delilah hops-skips-jumps over mushrooms
growing by the wood stove and
motions me forward, closer.
The house is wet and sagging,
a throbbing womb
electric and eclectic.
"Watch," she says, and so I do
and the spirits spin webs of gold and silver thread
around my hands and through my heart.
I smell turpentine and licorice
and touch the glittering thread to my lips
and whisper, "Oh."
Swamp smells old tires old wood old souls
dance and dance and dance and
Delilah, clapping smiling waving, shouts, "Write!"
and tosses confetti in the air. I catch it.
A sparkling handful of stars and

scatter it around me, a sacred circle,
and reach through veils of spiders' webs to nighttime sky
and shout, "I do, I do, I do."
I commit
To me. To you, Delilah.
I do.

II.

She come round here lot more than before.
She come round here with sirens in her eyes
rags wrapped round her throat
wrists long and bleedin' from the chains
she saw wrapped round them every day

She come round here lookin' for godknowswhat,
lookin' for whoknowswho —
sometimes I catch her eye when
I pass by a mirror or look out the
window when it's dark outside but
light as noon inside.

She come round here to snuggle deep
under your quilt as you lay with your new lover.
She come to slide between you
silent and slim
but solid,
separatin' you at the hips so you sleep apart
not even the soles of your feet touching.

She come round here to sit on the front porch
and rock with the wind with me waitin'
for the mail
me waitin' for the paper
waitin' for the preacher
me just waitin'.

She come round here to nuzzle up in your head
back behind your eyes in that place where
you do all your prayin'
that place where you do all your lyin'
that place where nobody but you knows the
real name of the spirit breathin' there.

She come round here to trace a trail
of perfume down the hallway
out into the kitchen and into the toolshed
where the two of you used to squeeze hard sweat
in the heat of the day.
Lady, oh, how I love to lay you down
mmhmmm, lady, oh.
She come round here to knock at the door
of your heart, slip in between your ribs and shake
you up like salad.
She come round here to wake you up and take you dancin'
naked feet leavin' footprints in the dewy grass
she come to give you dragonfly wings and colored chalk
to paint sidewalks inside out.
She come to kiss you gentle in the rain and
set your soul to flowin'.

Oh.

III.

Delilah want you to go down smooth like butter
She want you to hold your last whimper on your lips
until the final fragment blows away.
She want you to breathe free and easy like that song
and walk with bouncing steps even without your Nikes.
She want you to run barefoot over hot coals so you know
in the center of your self that you got no limits.
Nothing in your way
but you.

I want to honor the following people: Arvin Loudermilk and Mike Iverson for all their love and support over the last decade and for helping to make this possible for me. Carol Anne Perini for her constant love and friendship and inspiration, and Jeffrey Hartgraves for his wit, love, and invaluable editing advice. I honor Lynnsy Logue for her belief in my spirit and passion and her support of my truth.

And of course, my family. My mother, Elinor, for her love and friendship, belief, trust and infinite flexibility. My sister, Melanie, for believing in my dream in spite of herself, and my step-father, Keith, for his faith and support.

For Dad
who lit the spark

I miss you every single day.